"You haven't had much experience, and there's a lot to learn," Erin said.

"I was a cub scout," Patrick quipped. "I can tie knots like no other six-year-old."

"Up here it's not just about tying knots. And the weather can get ugly. It can blow you right off if you're not careful."

"I've got the balance of a mountain goat and a good grip. Do you have any boulders that need crushing?" Patrick raised his hands in menacing claws. Okay, so he was a joker. That didn't mean he was unqualified.

"People's lives are at risk. Sometimes we can't get to them in time—or at all," Erin said quietly. "Many of them didn't take the mountain seriously. We can't fall into that same mindset."

"Trust me, I understand," he replied.

Erin stuck out her hand again. "Welcome."

Patrick brightened and took her hand. "That's great! When do I start?"

"Tomorrow. I'll be your trainer," Erin said, surprising herself. But she wanted to see up close just what he could do...

Jennifer Brown is the award-winning author of young adult and middle-grade novels, including *Perfect Escape*, *Thousand Words*, *Torn Away* and the Shade Me series. Her acclaimed debut novel, *Hate List*, was selected as an ALA Best Book for Young Adults, a *VOYA* "Perfect Ten" and a *School Library Journal* Best Book of the Year, and her novel *Bitter End* was a 2012 YALSA Best Fiction for Young Adults. Her debut middle-grade novel, *Life on Mars*, was the winner of the 2017 William Allen White Children's Book Award.

Jennifer is also the nationally bestselling author of several women's fiction novels under the pseudonym Jennifer Scott. She lives in Kansas City, Missouri. Visit her at jenniferbrownauthor.com.

Rescue on the Ridge

JENNIFER BROWN

LOVE INSPIRED
INSPIRATIONAL ROMANCE

LOVE INSPIRED®
INSPIRATIONAL ROMANCE

Recycling programs
for this product may
not exist in your area.

ISBN-13: 978-1-335-42616-1

Rescue on the Ridge

Copyright © 2022 by Jennifer Brown

For questions and comments about the quality of this book, please contact us
at CustomerService@Harlequin.com.

Love Inspired
22 Adelaide St. West, 41st Floor
Toronto, Ontario M5H 4E3, Canada
www.LoveInspired.com

Printed in U.S.A.

And even to your old age I am he; and even to hoar hairs will I carry you: I have made, and I will bear; even I will carry, and will deliver you.
—*Isaiah* 46:4

For Scott

Acknowledgments

Just as Erin and Patrick must count on each other
and work together in rescue, so do I count on
my partners in writing rescue.

Thank you to Cori for so expertly leading me up the
mountain. You're always there with the gear that I
need, even if I sometimes need it because
I dropped mine during the hike (or, more likely,
left it in the car before we ever got started).

Thank you to the Love Inspired team for bringing in
the ropes and the helicopters and the walkie-talkies
so that I was safe on the mountain. And a special
thanks to my editor, Johanna Raisanen, for getting me
back down the mountain in one piece. Your support
and guidance are tireless, enthusiastic
and much appreciated.

Thank you to Love Inspired readers, who keep hope
alive that there will always be more mountains to
climb and that we will get to traverse them together.
You are wonderful hiking partners.

Thank you to my family for forever
and always coming to my rescue, regardless of
how I got stuck on the mountain in the first place.
I love you all the most.

And, finally, thank You to God for the mountains.
What gifts of Your glory they are.
I am honored to hike them.

Prologue

The girl was a sound sleeper. She wasn't one to jolt awake at the slightest creak of a settling house or a window scratch by the oak tree outside. Her bedroom door had a squeak, and even that didn't nudge her into consciousness. Had she been a light sleeper, maybe things would have been different.

She awoke slowly to an off-putting feeling, but when she swam into awareness and realized it wasn't just discomfort she felt, but a gloved hand over her mouth, it was too late. The gun was already pressed against her belly.

"One peep and you're dead." It was the voice of a stranger, a voice that filled her with dread and fear. Slowly, his form came into focus. Masked man, wearing all black, cloaked by the dark of her bedroom.

She found herself shaking her head—tiny, terrified shakes—and even she wasn't aware if she was telling him "no, don't do this," or if she was reassuring him. Making his job easier. Her mind searched for ways to alert her parents without screaming. There were none.

Her nostrils stretched wide, trying to allow in the air that her lungs begged for.

"You're going to get up, and you're going to come with us," the man said. "Do what we say, and we won't hurt you."

Us? We? Her eyes darted around the room until she picked out another form standing near her closed door. Another mask, another black outfit. What were the chances she could get away from two of them?

A tear slid from the corner of her eye and landed on her pillow as she absorbed that this was actually going to happen.

He lifted his palm from her mouth and moved the gun so it was pointing at her face, reminding her what power he really held over her. She was going to be his puppet.

She got out of bed and, grateful that she'd been chilly at bedtime and worn long sleeves, long pants and socks, stood in front of him. The other man rushed to her and grabbed both elbows, pulling them back behind her.

Trembling, Kerrington let her two captors lead her through the house quietly. They left through the laundry room window, which the man with the gun was careful to shut behind him.

It wouldn't be until someone tried to summon her for breakfast that anybody would know she'd been kidnapped.

By then, she would be long gone.

Chapter One

Erin Hadaway was parched. Ironic, given that she'd just spent most of the day kicking her crampons into thick ice, and there was a good chance the water bottle she'd left on the passenger seat in her truck was at least partially frozen. Winter had set in suddenly and fully, as it often liked to do in New Hampshire.

The couple she'd just rescued had been amiable enough, but were way too interested in levity to pay attention to the directions she was giving them. The woman had stepped on a loose rock in midquip, lost her footing and careened off the mountain, screaming.

Thankfully, Erin had already tethered her. The rope stopped the fall after only a few feet. The dangling woman had immediately burst into gales of delighted laughter, her husband joining in, while Erin's heart hammered in her throat. She'd never lost someone during a rescue, and she wasn't about to start now.

But for a moment there, it had looked possible.

She was glad to get them into Tommy's helicopter. She'd spent the rest of her hike back down to level ground just trying to settle her nerves.

She crunched over the gravel, her legs burning and her arms buttery warm and noodle-like. She shook them out as she walked, pulling crisp mountain air into her lungs. She'd been busy shutting down her landscaping business and adjusting to her new job at the plant nursery and hadn't been on the mountain in days.

Even though she'd been climbing for her whole life, getting up a mountain was still a workout. Especially when you added in the adrenaline of knowing that someone was counting on you to reach them as quickly as possible. How they had gotten to the ledge they were stranded on, or how they'd lost important pieces of their gear in the climb, didn't matter while she was on the mountain. All that mattered was that they were cold and hungry and had been there for a while.

Today's stranded couple had gotten to where they'd been because they wanted to take a picture. This happened a lot. The view, after all, was astonishing. After they'd snapped their photo, though, they realized they were stuck. Instead of losing their gear, they'd lost their nerve. Which also happened a lot. Getting back down a mountain wasn't nearly as fun as going up, and in some ways was twice as hard. People often found that they could fearlessly climb to a great height, but then became frozen with terror when it was time to descend. But Erin had a way of disarming people who'd lost their nerve. Her confidence was contagious.

Jason was good at that, too, she mused, then shook away the thought. It was impossible not to carry Jason's memory up the mountain with her, but she wanted desperately to leave it there. To stop carrying it everywhere she went.

She got to her truck and went straight for the water, which was, thankfully, still water. It wasn't nearly as cold on the ground as it had been up top, and now she could feel sweat trickling down her back. She pulled off her gear—ropes, carabiners, pickets—and dropped it into the toolbox in the bed of her truck, then shucked off her jacket, allowing the cold to push through the cotton of her T-shirt beneath.

Her phone rang. It was Rebbie, calling from the office. Rebbie didn't have an official title, but if she did, Erin supposed it would be Office Manager. Or maybe Person Who Runs the Entire Show Like It's No Big Deal would be closer to the truth. Or possibly just Best Human.

"You on flat ground?" Rebbie asked.

"Yeah, is Tommy?"

"Nope. As usual, you beat him." This had been Erin's most recent game—challenging herself to get down the mountain before Tommy could deposit his cargo and get back to the helipad. This time of year she would almost always win, as people tended to get stranded much farther down the mountain than they did during the warmer months. "You got time to stop in?"

Erin glanced at her watch. She wouldn't be wanted at the nursery for another couple of hours. "Yeah, sure. What's up? Please tell me it's not paperwork. You know I hate paperwork."

Rebbie laughed. "You can't escape the paperwork. But don't worry, I filled out most of it. You just need to write your report and sign. I'm actually calling because we've got a new volunteer."

"New volunteer? In the winter?" Presidential Aid, Rescue and Recovery—PARR—never got new volunteers in the winter. In the springtime, everyone wanted to get back in shape and thought mountain rescue would make for a good exercise routine. Few of them lasted long. Calls for rescue rarely happened at a convenient time, and nobody wanted to leave their baseball game or get out of their pajamas, no matter how good the cardio.

But winter was also a great time to train someone— if a climber could handle Mount Washington in the winter, they could handle anything.

"I told him it may be a bit before he would see any action, but he still wanted to sign up. And he's here, so I figured you'd want to meet him." There was a rustling, and then Rebbie whispered, "Trust me, you want to meet him."

Erin chuckled and rolled her eyes. Rebbie was relentless. "Oh, tell me, is he going to be *the love of my life*?"

"I mean, I wouldn't rule it out."

"Rebbie, how many times do I have to remind you that you need to stop trying to marry me off? I'm happy by myself."

More whispering. "Who said anything about marriage? I'm just saying you could do worse."

"Fine. I'll come in and say hi, but only because I have paperwork to sign. Don't get any ideas about proposing a double date or anything."

"Oh, I hadn't even thought about that. What a great

idea! James will be thrilled when I tell him to put on his going-out pants!"

"Don't you dare."

"I could just mention it…"

"Rebbie, I'm not joking…"

"I won't," she said with a laugh. "I promise. I'm not that mean. But a little pizza…a movie—it could be nice."

"Rebbie!"

"Okay, okay! But you'd better get here before I change my mind. He's super handsome."

"Uh-huh." There was no way Mr. Superhandsome Volunteer hadn't heard every bit of that conversation in the tiny PARR office. "This won't be awkward at all."

Erin hung up and jumped into the truck. She was still wearing her climbing helmet, the straps hanging loose at her temples. There'd been days she'd shown up for work at the nursery and only then realized she was still in climbing gear—her second skin.

As she drove to the office, she thought about how nice it would be to get a new climber, and what perfect timing this was. All she had right now were Rich and, on holiday weekends when he was home from college, Kevin. During the summer months, PARR often felt stretched thin. When she'd founded the volunteer group, she hadn't expected to become the group the local sheriff relied on the most. She also hadn't expected to lose Jason.

And she certainly hadn't expected to be doing what she was about to do. Nobody knew, because she still couldn't believe it herself. But she'd made the phone call just that morning; the ball was officially rolling.

The PARR office was near an airfield, not far from the base of the mountain. It was a tiny stand-alone building, not much bigger than a shed, and mostly housed an impressive communication setup, a file cabinet, a closet, a minuscule bathroom, two very creaky office chairs, a folding chair for visitors and a paper-strewn desk that Rebbie tried valiantly to keep clean. Erin didn't have the money for a huge building, and it hardly seemed necessary, anyway. The climbers were rarely all there at once, and even then were only there to mobilize and get up the mountain, which was more than big enough for everyone. She'd often thought of the entire Presidential Range as her office. Wasn't that what everyone wanted—an office with a view?

Erin parked next to a sparkling, brand-new pickup and went inside. She could hear the thrumming of Tommy overhead, making his way home. She cocked a thumb over her shoulder toward the airfield. "All good?"

Rebbie smiled. "Says he doesn't even think they'll have frostbitten toes. You broke time barriers, my friend." She turned to the man sitting in the folding chair. "She's a superhero."

Erin could feel herself blush. She hated being called out for anything in general, but she was especially not comfortable with effusive praise. She didn't rescue for the glory; she did it because people needed help, and because the mountain they needed help on had been her playground for almost her entire life.

Besides, superheroes didn't fail, did they? And she'd failed. Colossally.

"I don't know about that," she said. "Just a climber doing my job."

"Correction," Rebbie argued, handing Erin a stack of papers. "Her *job* is landscaping. So she saves people *and* the environment. *Super*. Hero."

"Wow!" The man stood and held out his hand. "Color me impressed."

"Don't be," Erin said, taking his hand. "She's making me sound way more valiant than I actually am. And I, um…shut down the landscaping business."

"You what?" Rebbie asked, but Erin pretended not to hear her.

"I'm Erin Hadaway." They shook, and Erin instantly noted that his hands were strong. She'd developed a theory over time that the softer a volunteer's handshake was, the less time they lasted at PARR. Sometimes people didn't even make it through the training, often quitting after the first rescue that was beyond basic. That was most rescues, really.

She locked eyes with the man, stricken by the cheerfulness in his gaze. His eyes were a deep, bottomless shade of brown, like melted chocolate, and had a certain merriness about them.

"Patrick Rogers. Great to meet you."

"I'll leave you to it," Rebbie said in a singsong voice, gathering her coat and purse from under the desk. "But don't think our conversation about your landscaping business is over. I need details. Patrick, it was nice chatting with you. I hope your project is a huge success."

"Likewise. And thank you." He held up a foam cup. "And thanks for the famous hot chocolate."

"*World*-famous," Rebbie corrected with a wink. She shrugged into her coat, whipped a scarf out of nowhere and expertly tossed it into place as she bolted. Erin watched as Rebbie made a beeline for Tommy and automatically knew she was delaying the pilot from coming inside and crashing what she certainly had convinced herself was going to be an instant love connection. Rebbie just couldn't stand the idea of a superhero being without a sidekick.

Alone in the office with Patrick, Erin suddenly felt self-conscious, like she was on a blind date. Weird… She'd never felt this way before, and Rebbie was more famous for her matchmaking attempts than she was for her hot chocolate—the secret was heavy cream and two melted squares of a Hershey's bar.

Erin had been on the receiving end of these matchmaking attempts more times than she could count. Usually, she felt exasperated and impatient, and only a handful of times had Rebbie's efforts ended in an actual date. Only twice had those ended in a second date. And only once had it ended in a relationship. Which eventually just…ended. In the year since Jason's passing, Rebbie had seemed to ramp up her efforts, as if a romantic night on the town could make Erin forget what had happened.

But there was something about Patrick that tugged at her. It wasn't just his strong hands and those hypnotizing brown eyes, nor was it the shadow of stubble that hugged his square jaw, the gold flecks that the sun picked out of his brown hair or the easy smile that showed off one slightly crooked canine...all of which flooded Erin with silly embarrassment over having even noticed them. Most notably, what caught her attention was a sure steadiness that made her think he would be one of the volunteers who stuck around. And there was something about that thought that she didn't mind in the least.

"So, " Patrick began, "you had a rescue today?"

Erin nodded, forcing herself to focus. "I'm sure my hands are freezing after being up on the rock."

"Not at all. Actually, they're really warm. Probably your head is warm, too, huh?" He patted the top of his own head.

Oh, no. The helmet.

Once again, she had forgotten she was wearing it. But unlike at the nursery, where she could rattle around in the greenhouse by herself all evening without a hair care in the world, now she was faced with a decision—leave it on, which would be totally awkward at this point, or take it off and deal with having a really bad case of sweaty helmet hair.

She went with the latter choice and hoped that running her fingers through her short hair would help fluff it up a little. She laid the helmet on the desk and gestured at the folding chair.

"Please, have a seat." Patrick sat, and she did the same. "So you want to be a rescuer."

"Yes."

"Do you have any climbing experience?"

"Some. I grew up in New Castle, so I'm familiar with the terrain."

Erin tried not to let her hopes about Patrick be

dashed at the words *New Castle*. In her experience, having grown up in New Castle meant he likely came from money, and compared to the rest of the volunteers, who were all local townies, he was probably from a wealthy family. She'd seen it time and again with volunteers from the cities near the coast. "I'm familiar with" meant "I've been on ski vacations."

She ventured a guess. "The Wildcat?"

He nodded. "Every winter since I was six. I was a ripper by thirteen. At least, I like to think so." Being a *ripper* meant that he was actually a pretty good skier—someone who didn't just ski down a mountain, but "ripped it up"—and that he'd probably done it enough to feel comfortable in the altitude, which was a plus.

"So you know how to come down. Any experience going up? I mean, without a ski lift?"

He made a guilty face. "It's been a few years. But I've climbed, yes. And I've done my fair share of avoiding getting mangled by trees on the way down. I figure that counts for something."

Erin chuckled. That probably did count for something.

"So you've never needed a rescue?"

He held up his palms and shrugged. "What can I say? I'm a natural." But she thought that for just a second, she saw a flicker of something serious try to blink across his face. Maybe she was just imagining it. "I'm doing some free-climbing now that I've moved to Gorham," he said. "Mostly bouldering. Just to get my footing."

Erin's gaze sharpened. "I live in Gorham. It's a far cry from New Castle. Must be a big change for you."

He shrugged. "It's a good change. I created a whole new development arm of our real estate business so I could move out here. We're going to develop a stretch of land just off the highway. Very convenient location. If, that is, I can get the owner to sell."

"Real estate? Oh—" It dawned on Erin that she'd seen Patrick's face before, on plenty of brochures. *Our real estate business* meant the Rogers Real Estate conglomerate. Huge. Loads of money. His father—or the man she guessed was his father—was one of the Top 30 Richest People in America. Patrick wasn't just wealthy; he was loaded.

As if he could feel her unease, Patrick sat forward in his chair. "Listen, I'm here because of the business, yes, but I could have chosen any number of places for this project. I chose Gorham for a reason." Again, she thought she could see—no, maybe *feel* was more accurate—a slight shift in him as he talked. *Desperation* wasn't the right word, but it wasn't far off.

"And that reason is…?"

He sat back again. "This may sound really… I don't know, sentimental or something? The mountain called to me. It's a calling."

This was something Erin could relate to. She, too, had felt called by the mountains. She'd felt it as far back as she could remember. Since birth, maybe, when she breathed her first lungful of crisp Appalachian air. One thing she loved about mountains was that they were forever—a mountain would never turn on you.

At least she'd thought that once upon a time. It certainly had turned on her when it came to Jason.

She cleared her throat, realizing she was dangerously close to being swept into a whole mess of memories that both warmed and hurt her.

"I guess that answers my next question, which was why do you want to be a rescuer?" She forced another tight smile, then focused on the papers in her hand, as if she was scrutinizing his application. "Anyway, winter is the best and worst time to start with PARR. It's good to get your feet wet, so to speak, while the weather is bad. And there aren't as many actual rescues, because all of the tourists are...well, they're on the Wildcat, *ripping*." She gave him a quick glance over the paperwork. "But on the other hand, the weather is bad and there aren't as many rescues."

"Two sides of the same coin," he said.

"Something like that, yes. I'm just telling you this because you haven't had much experience, and there's a lot to learn. And it's a hard time of year for learning."

"I'm a quick learner." He gestured toward the paperwork. "Dartmouth business school. Top of my class." Indeed, a quick check of the application verified that he did possess a business degree from the prestigious college. However, likely nothing he learned in college would be useful to him here.

"We do a decent amount of ropes rescue. I'm assuming you didn't take a ropes rescue course at Dartmouth?" The question came out sharper than she'd intended, and she instantly wanted to rewind the words right back into her mouth, but the comment didn't seem to faze him in the least.

"I was a Cub Scout for all of kindergarten," he quipped. "I can tie knots like no other six-year-old."

"Right. Of course, you know that up here it's not just about tying knots. And the weather can get ugly," she persisted.

"Looks don't matter to me. I prefer a good sense of humor in my weather, anyway."

"There will be lots of ice."

"I've been looking for a reason to buy an ice pick."

"The wind is brutal. The strongest winds in the States are up here. It can blow you right off of a hand-hold if you're not careful."

"I've got the balance of a mountain goat, and the grip of... Here, I'll show you. Do you have any boulders that need crushing?" He raised his hands as if they were menacing claws, which involuntarily plucked a chuckle out of Erin.

"You're funny," she said.

"I'll keep you entertained on the mountain," he said. "Another tick in the pros list. You haven't heard most of my repertoire. Believe it or not, it gets even better. I mean, it probably can't get any worse, right?"

"But you should know that the job is not fun and games. People's lives are at risk. Sometimes we can't get to them in time. Sometimes..." *One time in particular...* "Sometimes we can't get to them at all. Many of them end up in the position they're in because they weren't taking the mountain seriously. We can't fall into that same mindset. It could be deadly for everyone."

"Trust me," he said, instantly switching to an air of confidence that had the same force he'd projected with the humor. "I'll treat the job like God Himself sent me to do it."

Erin was taken aback. He had no way of knowing that this was exactly how she'd felt about her own mountain obsession for most of her life—like God had sent her there, and it was up to her to figure out why. And how she'd felt like she may be betraying God right now by doing what she was about to do: rebuke the mountain.

Her gut told her that Patrick might be a little deeper than he was projecting with the jokes. She could ignore her other reservations about him. And besides, she had a suspicion he was right about keeping her entertained during the climb.

She stood and stuck out her hand again. "Welcome to PARR."

He brightened and took her hand. "That's great! When do I start?"

"We can start training tomorrow. Be here at eight for paperwork, and then we'll head up. Dress warm, bring whatever gear you've got. We'll supply the rest for now, but if you decide you like it and want to stick with it—"

"I do. I will."

"You'll want to pick up some of your own things."

"Done."

"I'll be your trainer," she said, surprising herself with how seamlessly the words had come out of her mouth. Technically, Rich was the trainer for the beginners' orientation, and Erin didn't get new volunteers until they'd reached the more advanced training.

But for some reason, she wanted to see for herself what the real estate heir could do.

"Good." His grin disarmed her. "I was hoping you'd say that."

Chapter Two

After Patrick climbed into his truck and drove off, Tommy disentangled himself from Rebbie and came inside.

"Whew! Today's rescue..." He chuckled, shaking his head. "Can you imagine having to get rescued over a selfie?"

Tommy was older, retired from the US Air Force and probably the most likely candidate to run an organization like PARR in Erin's absence. He was incredibly young and spry for his age, and passionate about doing his part in the rescue. But Erin knew he wouldn't want to take over, if for no other reason than he wouldn't understand why she was asking in the first place. He would definitely try to talk her out of it. PARR was her baby.

"No, I can't," she said, lowering into her desk chair. She had time to knock out a little paperwork before her shift.

"Apparently they have a whole collection of what they called danger selfies. They run some sort of web-

site or something. They said this wasn't their first rescue." The more he talked about the couple they'd had
to pluck off the mountain today, the more agitated Erin
got. "I never would have thought there'd be an audience for that sort of thing. But I guess if they don't
mind getting into tight spots…"

"The mountain is no joke," she said, something
she'd repeated more times than she could count over
the last year. "It's not there to entertain fans of a web-
site. Danger selfies. How irresponsible. Getting into
tight spots is funny until you can't get out. And then
you put other people's lives in danger."

"True, true." Tommy got quiet and poured himself a coffee. He'd been around long enough to know
when to end a subject, Erin supposed, and then she felt
guilty that she was the reason subjects needed to end.
He sipped his coffee while staring out the window at
the weather-beaten PARR banner, which fluttered a
lively dance alongside the American flag. "Wind's getting worse," he said. "Gets much stronger and I won't
be able to go in for pickups. You know."

"Yeah," Erin said, shifting paperwork—always
with the paperwork—around on her desk. She fiddled
with her pen. She may have had the time, but she had
no motivation to actually fill out any of it. She didn't
know if she felt so unsettled because of the so-called
danger selfies, or because of the conversation with Patrick, or because of the thing she'd done that morning.
"I know. Hopefully it won't be needed."

"Rebbie tells me we've got a new guy."

Erin let out a short breath. "Speaking of not taking
the mountain seriously."

"Jokester, huh?"

"A real laugh a minute."

"Nerves, maybe. People make jokes at all sorts of uncomfortable times."

Erin dropped her pen and rubbed her forehead. She was starting to suspect it was all of those things rolled into one that had her out of sorts. She was doubting herself on just about every decision she'd made. "Rescues are uncomfortable times, don't you think?"

Maybe she shouldn't have trusted Patrick Rogers to be reliable on the mountain. She knew the type— he was so used to charming his way into anything he wanted, he began to believe that he could do anything. Not true. Not when it came to emergency situations. She worried that she'd been taken in by him, and that possibility annoyed her even more. She wasn't used to being taken in by anyone.

Tommy nodded. "Usually they are uncomfortable times, yes. The selfie-takers today seemed to be in pretty high spirits, though."

"Well, I'm glad neither of them died for their audience's amusement. Would have been a real shame if I hadn't been available for the rescue and they died on a lark, now, wouldn't it?" The office suddenly felt too tiny. Cramped. Hot. Erin immediately felt guilty for snapping at Tommy. He didn't do anything to deserve it. She picked up her helmet. "I'm sorry, Tommy. I appreciate you so much. I just… I need to go."

Tommy eyed her over his cup. "You know, nobody thinks what happened to Jason was your fault."

"Yeah, of course, I know that. I just need to get to the nursery."

"Erin…"

"Sorry I'm such a grouch. It's not you, I promise." She patted his shoulder. "I really do have to get to work, though."

"There was nothing you could have done."

She pretended she didn't hear the last as she pushed her way into the wind. In a year of telling herself that, she still couldn't quite convince herself it was true. What would make him think she would believe it when he said it now?

Her pickup rattled as she navigated away from the mountain and toward the highway that would take her into town. She passed a billboard—Rogers Real Estate Coming Soon—and frowned. This must be Patrick's project that he was in town to work on. Right now it was just a sign on a bare field. He would be in Gorham for a while. Enough time to learn the ropes, so to speak, and maybe get a rescue or two in before jetting back to the coast, adventure fulfilled.

Just don't let him kill anyone in the process. Including himself.

She pulled into her driveway and checked her watch. She still had an hour before she had to be at the nursery. Plenty of time to change clothes and visit Roberta. She opened her garage door and quickly transferred her gear onto tidy shelves, then went inside and traded her climbing clothes for jeans and a thick sweater. She ran a brush through her hair and swiped on a little clear lip gloss. Her bloodhound, Murphy, nosed at her leg for attention.

"Hey, buddy," she said, reaching down to give his ears a good scratch. Murphy had been through everything with Erin. He understood what was happening with her. Old Murph's floppy ears were the best listening ears in the world.

Erin's kitchen showed signs of a life interrupted. It was a common aesthetic for her house—tasks half-finished, meals half-cooked, a sink full of tepid dishwater with any trace of bubbles long gone. Sometimes she would come back from a rescue to find the TV still on, the remote sitting next to her full mug of now-cold coffee. She learned early on that she couldn't live life always afraid to do anything for fear of being interrupted, but she could hardly make someone wait while she caught up on the morning news. It was a balance she'd perfected over the years.

She poked at the blueberry muffins she'd baked that morning. They'd gone uncovered while she was on the mountain, but still seemed to be pretty fresh, giving way under her touch. A quick zap in the microwave and a slather of butter, and they would be good as new. She tossed four muffins into a bag and slid into her shoes.

"Be right back, Murph," she said as she headed out. "No parties while I'm away."

Erin's next-door neighbor, Roberta, was standing at her front door, as if she'd been waiting for Erin to arrive. Maybe she had been. Life could get awfully lonely for the elderly widow, especially on days like today, when the weather was turning bleak. Erin's visits were sometimes the only human contact Roberta had all day.

"Oh, goodness, the wind," Roberta said, holding

the door open for Erin with one hand and the neck of her sweater closed with the other. "Hurry, hurry!"

"I'm afraid I don't have a ton of time today." Erin held up the bag of muffins. "Just enough time for one of these. Maybe two. I've worked up an appetite."

"I'll get the butter," Roberta said, leading Erin to the kitchen. "How's the mountain today?"

"One rescue, pretty easy. Got down before that front started moving in." Erin took two plates and a knife to the table, then went back for two glasses and some milk.

"Thank goodness for that. I worry about you getting blown away like a kite with those high winds."

Erin chuckled. "You and me both. I'll be back up there tomorrow. Wind or no wind."

Roberta paused, turned and raised her eyebrows. "Surely not. What on earth for?"

"Training a new guy. It's the best time, if he wants to know what he's getting into."

The widow returned to her task. "If you say so."

They met at the table and sank down across from each other, the muffins on a plate between them, a well-coordinated ballet. There were times that Roberta's bustling energy in the kitchen reminded Erin of her mother, always busy kneading or mixing or pounding or frying, their tiny kitchen flooded with sunlight, "because sunshine is free, and only fools turn away God's free gifts." Sometimes, when Erin most missed her mother, these moments in Roberta's kitchen were exactly what she needed.

They bowed their heads, and like always, Roberta said a quick prayer.

"Dear Lord, thank You for this food, and for the friendship and company of my lovely neighbor, Erin. Thank You for giving her the ability to help so many people in their time of great need. And thank You, Lord, for helping her heal in *her* time of need, too. Amen."

She always ended her prayer that way—*thank You for helping her heal*—but Erin didn't feel healed. Not at all. In fact, she felt like she had a whole lot more healing to go and wasn't sure if the Lord was going to see her all the way through.

That was why she'd made the decision she had that morning. The decision she needed to tell Roberta about.

She echoed Roberta's "amen," but it felt stuck in her throat.

Roberta dug in right away, but Erin's appetite had suddenly diminished. She hated keeping secrets. She had to get this over with.

She pulled a folded flyer out of her back pocket and laid it on the table between them. Roberta glanced at it and then did a double take.

"What's this?"

Erin slid the flyer closer to Roberta's reach. Roberta set down her fork and picked up the paper, unfolding it in her shaky hands. She pushed up her glasses and gave it a good study.

"Smythe Realtors," she read, and then she turned her watery eyes to Erin, a question in them that broke Erin's heart. "You're moving?"

"I haven't put it officially on the market yet, but… yes." Erin poked at her muffin with her fork. She felt sick.

Roberta laid down the flyer. "But your landscaping business…"

"I've already shut it down for the season," Erin said. "I'll just reopen in the spring…somewhere else."

"Somewhere else in Gorham?"

Erin shook her head, feeling the weight of Roberta's disappointment all the way down to her toes. Who was going to look after her with Erin gone? She had a moment of déjà vu, her mother standing at the front door, holding a kitchen towel in one hand, waving goodbye with the other, looking so small and mystified as Erin pulled away, the only one of her seven children to leave the holler. "No, not in Gorham. Somewhere…farther."

"How far?"

"I'm not sure yet. Maybe the Midwest."

"What about your rescue group?"

"I'll leave it in good hands. Competent hands. Rebbie and Tommy will keep it running smoothly. Maybe Rich will want to take over. Kevin's a little young, but we've got this new guy and he may want to—"

"Oh, honey." Roberta reached over and laid her hand on top of Erin's. "This won't bring Jason back, you know."

Erin paused. She'd known she was babbling, which was something she often did when she was overcome with emotion. First Tommy and now Roberta—the second time in less than an hour. She must have really been wearing her grief on her sleeve today. "I know. But I can't keep looking at that mountain. I can't keep going up there. What if…? What if I have to go to the…? What if I have to see…?" She couldn't finish the sentence.

"My guess is you've been seeing it in your head every day since it happened."

A tear slipped out without Erin even realizing she'd been close to crying. As usual, Roberta had hit the nail right on the head. For a moment, Erin was seized with the thought that she couldn't possibly move away—not because Roberta needed her, but because she needed Roberta.

"Oh, dear," Roberta said and patted her hand again. "Just do a little praying on it before you make a final decision. Will you at least promise me that much?"

"Of course."

"Good. Now let's stop talking about this. Tell me about today's rescue."

Erin wiped her eyes, took a deep breath and picked up her fork, grateful for the subject change. "Do you know what a selfie is?"

Two muffins and twenty minutes later, Erin was officially running behind. Her head felt as heavy and full as her muffin-stuffed belly. She had a lot of thinking and praying to do. As she drove to work, she felt very grateful that Dan and Lila, the husband and wife team who'd hired her at the nursery, were understanding people. They gave her a lot of grace when it came to her work schedule. But she hated leaning on that grace. She'd felt like she bumbled her way into the job and had been bumbling ever since.

Unless she made this move, she feared she would be bumbling forever.

Chapter Three

Patrick could have asked for his rescue training to start after work. Or on Saturday. He was pretty sure that Erin Hadaway would have accommodated his schedule. But the truth was, he was happy to skip the virtual board meeting. He was happy to cancel his lunch with the architect. And he really didn't mind missing the phone conference with his father.

He felt free on days like this one. They were few and far between. Days when he could be a *person*, rather than an *heir*. Being an heir to Rogers Real Estate was exhausting and stuffy and everything he was not. His heart was adventurous and full of excitement and wonder—his job was stagnant and boring and predictable.

But he'd shut down his heart fifteen years ago, on a day that he would never forget. He'd decided it was time to grow up, and to him, at that time, growing up meant giving in, officially becoming Patrick Harold Rogers III, the person he swore he would never be. Ever since, he'd been obediently following marching orders, as if he was six instead of thirty-six, and wishing he could just experience something. Anything. The birth of Patrick Harold Rogers III had coincided with the death of his dreams, but it was a death that would forever be overshadowed by the other true devastation he'd brought onto the family.

All an accident, of course. But an accident that reshaped everything and redirected his course from passion to purpose. To obligation and obedience.

But fifteen years was a long time of longing. He just wasn't sure he could do it anymore.

Pastor Elmer really was the one who'd gotten things started with a sermon that Patrick felt deep in his bones. So deep that he asked to speak with the pastor privately afterward, to make sure he understood the message. A fire had been lit under him.

So when the opportunity to start a project in Gorham opened up, Patrick had jumped on it. And even though his father had objected, said it was beneath his position, Patrick remained steadfast. He saw it as his chance to step outside himself, to remember who he was at his core. It wasn't until the drive into Gorham, as he saw the mountain grow enormous in his windshield, that he realized it was also his moment for atonement. He'd prayed for direction, and God had led him right back to the path where he'd lost his way. It made sense.

In that moment, he'd fought an urge to stop and unhook the trailer from his truck. Let his belongings go, buy a sleeping bag and tent, and just live in the trees. Prove that he could.

He didn't end up going that far. But eating Cheerios

in a cozy little kitchen before gearing up to climb the mountain with—he would be the first to admit—a very captivating rescue trainer was close enough… for now.

His phone rang. His mother.

"Hi, Mom!" Cheery. Energetic. Hopeful.

"Patrick." Reserved. Mistrustful. Slightly disgusted. The usual. "Are you settling in?"

He took the last bite of his cereal and tucked his phone between his shoulder and ear while he took the bowl to the sink. "Yeah, I am. It's beautiful here. And I've already begun making progress on the land. I met with the survey—"

"Stop. You know I don't talk business. That discussion is for your father."

"Right." He ran water into his bowl, trying to ignore the feeling of his energy running right down the drain with it. As usual, just hearing his mother's voice brought his guilt front and center. He felt a tingle of doubt niggling around in the back of his brain. "How are things at home?"

She sighed. "Nothing's changed, of course. You've not been gone a month."

"Right," he said again.

"You'll be coming home next weekend, though," she said. Not a question, but a demand. Yet another expectation for Patrick Harold Rogers III.

"Next weekend?"

"It's the anniversary."

Silence stretched between them. He turned off the water and heard the hiss and gurgle of the coffeepot finishing a brew on her end. Like they were having breakfast together, one hundred miles apart. Which, to be fair, was how it would feel even if they were sitting in the same room together back in New Castle. "Right," he said for the third time. "About that…"

"As you know, it's tradition for us to celebrate and remember on that day. I've got painters working on the bathroom this morning. Did you know that there's a difference between balmy blue and rhythmic blue? It's just the tiniest difference, but now that I've seen it, I can't stand for balmy blue to be on those walls for another second. I can't possibly have guests here with it looking like that. Of course, we will have to upgrade the tile if we upgrade the paint. You know how these things snowball. I'm not sure if we can get it all done before next weekend, but I'm going to see how much a rush job would cost, just in case. And I found this little golden elephant—trunk up, of course, because you know how she always insisted that her elephant figurines have an upward trunk—"

"Yes, I remember," Patrick said, leaning against the counter. "Mom, I don't think I can make it this time."

She gave another disgusted little sigh. "Now is not the time for jokes, Patrick. I have things to do. I've got to call the caterers. See if they can make mints in the shape of elephants, actually. Don't you think that would be a good idea?"

"Mom—"

"Maybe an elephant-shaped cake."

"Mom." She fell silent. The kind of silence that tore at Patrick. The kind where she expected the worst of him, just because the worst was all she could see.

"We do this every year," she finally said.

"I know."

"I would think that you, of all people, would want to be there."

He squeezed his eyes shut. There it was—the *you of all people* that would hit him in his core, steal his breath away, steal his will away. *You of all people* was what kept him in a boring family job that he didn't want to be in. It was what kept him from forgiving himself and living his own life.

The truth was, he had no real reason not to be there, other than that he was in Gorham and it all felt too real, as if he had been transported fifteen years into his past. He was at the base of the beast and planned to make amends, once and for all. With the mountain, with himself, with the past…and with his sister. He realized only now, through the sound of his mother's small, afraid voice, that not coming home next weekend would be cruel. "Okay," he said. "Sure. I'll be there."

"As I suspected," she said.

He checked the time. "I've got to go."

"Your father said you canceled some meetings today."

"Yeah, uh, I have a thing. Some training. Rescue stuff."

This time the silence was complete. No coffee maker gurgling out its last few drops, no appalled hitch in his mother's breath. It was only broken by the click of the phone disconnecting. She'd hung up. He winced. He would not take it personally. On some level, he felt he deserved it. He should have known she would react that way.

He put away his phone and focused on getting dressed, snapping tags off of new clothes and pulling stickers off of new gear. He hoped that Erin Hadaway had extras of the things he'd neglected to buy.

He stepped outside and instantly curled in on himself against the wind. He probably should have concentrated less on carabiners, which he knew he had given an overinflated sense of importance because of their appearance in many action movies and the satisfying click when they were attached, and focused more on protection against the cold. His jacket wasn't going to cut it. He would freeze up there.

Yesterday, when he left the PARR office, he'd been too worried about the chill he'd encountered inside the office to realize how much the temperature had dropped outside. The wind had ripped and clawed against his truck, so that he had to pay attention to keep from being pushed from the road altogether. It was as if winter wasn't just arriving, but was barreling in on them headfirst, like a comic book supervillain. Overnight, the air had turned frigid.

He only hoped Erin Hadaway had thawed a little.

He definitely had a feeling she'd been offended by him. Not by something he said or did, but by his very existence. She hadn't started out that way. In fact, at first, he thought he detected the slightest spark of chemistry between them. But as the interview went on, she closed down on him, bit by bit. It was like watching someone pull the shades on every window of a house, one by one.

She made him nervous, which never happened. Like his father constantly reminded him, it was hard to be nervous when you were the most competent person in the room. Or something like that. Sometimes he wasn't sure where his actual competence ended and his competent persona began. His biggest fear was one day discovering that he was all persona.

Yet another problem with being an heir—you had no chance to figure out what you were actually good at.

Patrick would've been a fool not to notice that Erin Hadaway was beautiful. She was athletic and lean. According to Rebbie, she knew everything there was to know about mountain climbing and scrambled up and down the rocks as handily as walking down a sidewalk. Rebbie had told him that Erin had grown up in the mountains, but she hadn't said which ones. He could detect a slight accent beneath Erin's words—just a softening at their tail ends that hinted of the South and delighted him.

He wanted to know more about Erin.

But she was pretty closed off, and he couldn't tell if that was who she was, or if that barrier was just for him. He suspected the latter.

The PARR parking lot was empty when he arrived. He was early. He anxiously drummed his thumbs against his steering wheel while he waited for someone to arrive, and then practically launched himself out of his truck when Rebbie's car pulled in next to him. She held back a smirk as she watched him fumble his way out of the driver's seat, as things fell off his pack and a couple of hooks got caught in the seat belt. She took her time gathering her things, and they emerged into the gusting wind at the same time.

"Good morning!" he called. "Beautiful day for a hike!"

"Hmm, I'm not so sure about that," she answered. The wind threatened to whisk away their words. But that only made him more excited to start climbing. It was the same sort of excitement that he'd once felt for the slopes—an adrenaline rush combined with a tiny knot of tension in the pit of his stomach. A particularly forceful gust of wind whipped past them, causing Rebbie to clamp her hand down on her stocking cap and squeeze her entire face into a squint. "Let's start with coffee."

The office was a blanket of warmth that instantly cut off winter when they stepped inside. Rebbie hurried over to the corner and turned on a space heater.

"Brrr, I would not want to be out in that today," she said. "Hard to believe anyone would. You know it gets worse as you get closer to the sky, right? Fewer obstacles to block that wind."

He chuckled and clapped his gloved hands together. "I'm counting on it. That's how you learn, right?"

She shook a finger at him. "Erin is going to like you."

He felt doubtful about that, based on the vibe he got from Erin during their interview. "Let's hope you're right," he said. "I don't want her to toss me off the mountain."

"She's only tossed two or three trainees off the mountain. You should be relatively safe, as long as you don't make her mad." She waited a beat. "Kidding! Kidding! She's more into the business of keeping people from being tossed off the mountain." She pulled off her hat, her hair sticking up in staticky wisps, and dropped it on the desk, then grabbed the coffeepot and took it into the bathroom to rinse and refill. "Honestly, I'm kind of surprised she's willing to take you up in this weather." She reappeared and dumped the water into the coffee maker. "She hasn't really been herself lately."

As if on cue, a truck barreled into the parking lot and skidded to an abrupt stop. Erin climbed out of it, looking stressed and frazzled. She jogged to the building.

"Sorry," she said by way of greeting. "I had a meeting."

Rebbie raised her eyebrows at Patrick as if to say, *See what I mean?*

"It's perfectly all right," Patrick said. Erin's coat was unzipped and she wasn't wearing a hat, yet she didn't seem the least bit cold. Her cheeks were even flushed, which he guessed was from the rush of running late. He found himself somewhat mesmerized by the way her rosy cheeks and short dark hair provided a frame for her eyes, which were a striking blue and ringed by the thickest, longest eyelashes he'd ever seen. Everything about this girl screamed *natural beauty.* "We were just making coffee. Well…*she* was making coffee. I was just standing here trying to get the feeling back in my fingers."

The tiny building shuddered with the wind, the blinds rattling against the window frame.

"I was thinking maybe he should wear a full suit," Rebbie said. "We have extras."

Patrick saw a startled expression flicker across

Erin's face, but then she nodded. No agreement or disagreement, just silent acquiescence. She peered through the window, but it was as if she was looking far off, rather than at the snowy mountain stretching out in front of them.

"I can run out and buy one," he offered.

Rebbie waved a hand at him. "Don't be silly. We have loads of them. I'm sure we have one your size. Here." She bustled to the little closet, rooted around for a few seconds, then came back out with a bright orange snowsuit. "This one should work."

He took the snowsuit, which felt incredibly light on the hanger, making him wonder if it would actually be warm enough against that wind, and stepped into it.

When he finished—instantly warm, by the way— Erin was standing by the closet holding a bright orange snowsuit of her own.

"Ready," he said, the word fluttering into a fit of nerves that grew in the pit of his stomach. He thought he might even be shaking a little. His sister's face floated just out of his mind's reach…and he wanted to keep it that way.

He *needed* to keep it that way.

Chapter Four

Rebbie had been right about the snowsuit—Erin knew this—but still, there was something about seeing Patrick in Jason's old gear that grated on her. Jason had taken the mountain very, very seriously. So much more seriously than a comedian weekend warrior who boasted about keeping her company on the hike.

She didn't need company; she needed safety.

She needed Jason back. He was her best friend, almost like a brother. And maybe that was what grated on her the most—someone else wearing his suit was the final confirmation that he was never going to wear it again.

That was hardly Patrick's fault. So why did she feel so angry at him?

"The wind can get really wicked," Rebbie whispered while Patrick climbed into the suit. "You don't want him getting hypothermia up there."

"I know," Erin whispered back. She stepped into her snowsuit as easily as slipping into a second skin. "It's fine. Really." But she knew that her face belied what she was saying. Nothing about this morning had been fine.

She'd met with the Realtor first thing in the morning. As she wandered with the woman, ticking off all the sweet little touches she'd put into her home with her own two hands, her resolve to sell had begun to fade. She'd followed like a protective mother bear, ready to swoop in and roar at the first sign of danger, all the while knowing that it had already passed.

She'd dragged the meeting on, stalling before showing the basement, the garage, the shed, the tiny cove off the kitchen that she liked to think of as her "thinking room." Next thing she knew, she was late and flustered and irritated.

And then Rebbie had to offer up Jason's clothing without even asking her. This was too much moving on all at once.

"He had a dozen of them," Rebbie whispered.

"I know," Erin said again.

"He wouldn't mind."

"I know. That doesn't mean I have to like seeing this guy wear it."

She had to admit, though, when Patrick finally got himself all tucked in and zipped up and ready to go, his face was little-boy excited. His smile was wide and welcoming, and she couldn't help adopting his anticipation. She thought he might have even been shaking a little. Jason would have liked Patrick.

They went through his pack piece by piece, and Erin was pleasantly surprised by all the gear that he'd brought with him. He was smart and seemed to instinctively know what basics he needed. *Ripper*, she reminded herself. *Rich ripper.* Just because he could throw money at the mountain didn't mean he knew what he was doing on it.

She loaded him up with some additional pulleys and anchors and a good bivvy bag, just in case he should need some shelter, then showed off PARR's TTRS system, which she loaded into her own pack. She grabbed two pickaxes and handed him one.

Finally, all geared up and sweating inside their suits, they climbed into her truck and hit the road, the first several minutes filled with awkward silence.

"We're going to hike the Traverse," she said, breaking the quiet. "Spans every peak in the range. It'll help you get a layout in your head. Don't worry—we won't do it all today. Just some. Hopefully we'll get to Mount Washington, but…" She leaned forward and peered up at the sky. She couldn't even see the top of the mountain for the clouds sitting so low on it. But she didn't need to see the top to know it would be snow- and ice-packed, slippery and dangerous. "Well, it's just not going to be easy on a day like today."

"But the brochure promised me easy," Patrick complained in a joking tone.

Erin forced a chuckle, because she thought that was what he was going for. But it was a hollow chuckle, one that got stuck in her throat behind a big block of dread. Getting to Mount Washington would mean passing Tuckerman Ravine. She hadn't done that in… well, almost a year.

"I've watched videos," Patrick said. "A lot of people give up."

Erin flicked her eyes to him. "Yes. I know. PARR is what happens when people give up."

"Oh. Right. I didn't think about that."

"We don't have the luxury of giving up. If you think you're a giving-up kind of person—"

"I'm not."

"Okay." A pause, then she added, "Good."

They rode the rest of the way to the trailhead in silence, and Erin could tell that she'd broken his good spirits. Guilt pushed in on her. She was starting to think she was punishing Patrick simply because he wasn't Jason.

"I'm sorry," she mumbled as they unfastened their seat belts. "I didn't think you would give up. I've just had a rough morning."

They pulled their gear out of the bed of the truck and loaded up. Erin couldn't help thinking about that Realtor as she pulled on her gloves and strapped on her pack. What had bothered her most was that the woman had looked at her home like it was simply a house. She'd scanned it like she was ticking items off a grocery list. She didn't know all the love that went into it—into Erin's entire existence here.

"Do you always go up with this much gear?" Patrick asked, ripping her out of her thoughts. She'd almost forgotten he was even there.

"Depends on why I'm going up," she said. "Different situations call for different gear. Since the weather is far from ideal, I'm being extra safe."

The truth was, she found the weight of the extra gear comforting. Growing up in the holler, she'd often climbed barefoot, scrambling from rock to rock as easily as walking from one end of the house to the other. Her granddad used to joke that she was part mountain goat and gave her the nickname Hooves.

There were times when she was so light, she felt as if she might float right off the mountain and into Heaven itself. She could remember a day or two, while nursing a broken heart or smarting from an argument, kneeling atop a peak and praying for just that. Not to die, but only to experience the weightlessness of Heaven for just one day.

The first time she'd gotten a call that a man had fallen on the Madison and was severely injured, leaving a sobbing little boy and an anxiously pacing golden retriever at the top of the cliff he'd fallen over, she realized that these mountains were not the gentle slopes of her childhood. The mountains in Kentucky were old friends; these mountains were…opponents.

And sometimes opponents won.

But she had to—*had to*—put that out of her mind.

"Ready?" Erin asked. Patrick nodded.

They took off up the trailhead, their crampons crunching over the snow-covered rock. There were a few footprints tracking ahead of them, but they were mostly snowed over. Erin wondered if whoever had made them had finished their hike safely, or if she and Patrick might run across an actual situation on their way. She twisted the volume knob on her two-way radio just in case Rebbie made a call.

"Heading up," she said into the radio.

Rebbie's voice came back, small and staticky. "Gotcha, boss. Remember, what goes up—"

"Must come down," Erin said and then clipped the radio to her belt. "Don't worry, we will."

Patrick chuckled. "Let's just hope we come down feetfirst."

"From your lips to God's ears," Erin said. They'd been walking at such a fast clip, they were already surrounded by trees. "We'll be going off-trail some. People like to get stranded in weird spots. Plus, I have a couple things to show you."

"Gotcha, boss. Going up," Patrick said. He was quick-witted, Erin would definitely give him that.

"So tell me what exactly it is that you do," Erin said, her lungs doing what they did naturally—stretching her breath in and out, slowly and steadily, oxygenating her limbs, her mind. "At your family's business, I mean."

"Ah," Patrick said. His breath was much more labored as they ascended, but Erin had come to expect that out of new volunteers. Jason had been the worst of them—they'd had to stop to rest four times on their first ascension, causing Erin to wonder aloud if he was certain mountain rescue was the endeavor for him. She'd had no idea he would ultimately turn out to be one of her best climbers. "I'm afraid you'll be so enraptured by the excitement of it all, you'll get distracted and we'll be lost on this mountain forever."

"That boring, huh?"

"Dreadfully boring," he said. "Unless you find filling out forms to be riveting. If so, then I've got story upon story for you."

Erin wasn't surprised by this. Her idea of work always involved sinking her fingers into dirt, feeling the breath of wind in her hair. If she had to spend her days crammed into an office—or worse, a cubicle— she might actually die of boredom.

"It's a family business," he continued. "My grand-father started it in the 1800s. Was the first to develop in ten cities on the East Coast."

"Wow, that's pretty impressive."

"It is," he agreed. "But was also probably way more exciting back then than it is now. My dad still works for the company, but he plans to retire in a few years, and then it becomes mine. Where's the confetti?"

"I take it you don't want that?"

"Not even a little bit."

"Why not?"

"It's just a bunch of cloud-regarding."

"Cloud-regarding? I'm sorry, I don't follow."

They were silent while they hoisted themselves up a particularly steep grade. Erin veered off into the woods, striking out for her first little treat—a jutting rock that hovered over a spectacular view and made you feel a little like you were standing on thin air.

"Cloud-regarding is just a term I picked up recently. Let's say I'm not what you would call passionate about the work," Patrick said when the land leveled out. Erin slowed her gait a bit to let him catch his breath. She knew another steep incline was coming up on them. "It's a bunch of forms and phone calls. Wheeling and dealing. Staring at clouds rather than, you know, doing things that matter."

"Why do you do it, then?"

"I don't really have a choice," he said.

She paused, turned to face him. "Everyone has a

choice." But even as it came out of her mouth, she knew that was a lie. She knew when she got home that night, the Realtor's perfume would still be lingering in the air, and she would be reminded of her own lack of choices.

Not true, she argued with herself. *You've made all kinds of choices. This is just the consequence of them.*

"Not when you're from my family," Patrick said, thankfully distracting Erin from her own thoughts. He gave a simple grin that told her she needed to move on to another subject. "And not when you're me."

She pressed forward, always listening for the crunch of Patrick's shoes behind her. They came up on a jutting rock and she scrambled to its top, then turned around, arms spread wide.

"Tuna Tears Rock," she announced.

"What?" Patrick asked.

"It's the name of this rock," Erin said. "I once had a rescue call from here. A mother and teen daughter had gotten lost in the woods, even though the signs clearly tell you to stay on the trail. Anyway, when I got here, they were sitting right here on this rock eating tuna fish sandwiches. The daughter was crying her eyes out, convinced they would never be found. So I took my old partner here during his training and told him the story, and he named this rock Tuna Tears. Come on up."

She scooted to the side so Patrick could join her, and he did with ease. They stood shoulder to shoulder as they looked out over the landscape.

"Wow," he said. "This is incredible. I feel like I'm—"

"Floating? I know." She was pleasantly surprised by how easy it was climbing with Patrick. He was agile and willing and didn't seem to have any fear.

"Yes, exactly," he said. "I dub this rock Floating Rock, formerly known as Tuna Tears."

And just like that, her happiness was gone. She bristled, despite herself. She knew that what happened to Jason wasn't Patrick's fault. But she couldn't listen to Patrick try to undo anything that Jason had done while he was up here. Jason had left every part of himself on this mountain—Patrick couldn't take that away.

She turned and hopped off the rock, then trudged a few paces away. "We should get going."

"Oh…okay," he said. She could tell from the sound of his voice that he was confused by her abrupt switch in mood. She didn't blame him. She was confusing.

What had happened was confusing.

Life was confusing.

So she needed to go to the place where she often went when she was confused. She needed to go to church.

Chapter Five

"We'll head back to the trail now," Erin said. "Our next stop isn't until we get to the other side of Adams. We'll head off-trail again at that time, go down into the notch."

Patrick dutifully followed behind her, and she could sense confusion and hurt coming from him. She hadn't been fair. She seemed to be specializing in that lately. Bumbling, bumbling, bumbling. She took a deep breath and tried again.

"So you don't like the family business, but you have to take it over."

"Huh? Oh. Yeah. It won't be so bad, though. Once I'm in charge, I'll just schedule a lot of golf meetings. Maybe branch out, into a whole new direction of building golf communities. That way it'll be research. Plus, I'll have PARR to keep me grounded."

"*Grounded* is an interesting word choice," Erin said, gesturing in front of her, where the trees opened up to show that they were approaching a peak. They'd peaked the Madison already. As if to prove her point, a gust of wind rushed at them. She bent her knees to brace against it, but Patrick took a couple of unsteady steps backward.

"Wow. This wind is something else."

"The worst wind gusts in the country happen up here," she said. "Particularly on the Washington. People who don't research before they plan their hikes learn that real fast." They paused a moment to appreciate the beauty of their position on the planet, then plunged onward.

"What about you?" Patrick asked to Erin's back. "What keeps you grounded?"

"Me? Oh, um…" She was shocked to learn that she didn't really have an answer. She could tell him what had once kept her grounded. She could pinpoint the exact moment she'd become ungrounded. But what currently kept her grounded? She had no idea. "This, of course."

"I guess that makes sense," he said. "Up here, you have to stay grounded, or you might find gravity grounding you."

"Something like that," she said. "I grew up in a Kentucky holler, so I guess you'd say nature grounds me. I'm an outdoors girl." Erin pointed to a dense grove of trees in the distance between the two mountains. "Our next stop is right down there."

"Off-trail again," Patrick said.

Erin nodded. "And a little more challenging than the last one."

Patrick clapped his gloved hands together. "Let's do it! I can't wait to hear what this place is named. Maybe Grouper Giggles Point?"

Erin couldn't help chuckling. While the name was outlandish, it was exactly the kind of joke that Jason would have come up with.

They veered off-trail again and plunged back into the woods. The descent was steeper here, and Erin's legs finally began to simmer into the low and slow burn that she loved. Her cheeks, meanwhile, were numb, and she paused to pull up her gaiter, motioning for Patrick to do the same.

Erin often said that one moment of distraction could make the difference between life and death on the mountain, and in this moment, she almost proved herself right.

Distracted by the gaiter, she took a wrong step.

At first, it seemed salvageable. She corrected for the step, her arms wheeling to regain her balance, but her momentum was thrown off. She took the next step too quickly, too forcefully, and all of her weight was on that foot. Down she went.

The grade was steep. And there was a drop-off just a few feet in front of them. It would dump her about twenty feet if she went over it. Depending on how she landed, she could be severely injured...or killed.

Erin had fallen while on mountains before. She knew how to arrest a slide. But she'd been holding her pickaxe and had, astonishingly, dropped it in her fall. She grabbed for it, but couldn't maneuver herself quickly enough. The pickaxe skittered just out of her reach, hit a groove and tumbled end over end until it was stopped by a tree.

She was only feet from the drop-off. She started to panic.

She knew better than to dig her feet or toes into the ground to stop herself. It was a great way to break an ankle. But she was looking at either a broken ankle or broken everything. She flipped with a grunt, starfished, pulled her knees in toward her stomach and planted her crampons into the snow.

If the incline had been softer, the ground smoother, she might have pulled it off. But it was neither of those things, and the instant inertia sent her tumbling end over end, just like her pickaxe had done.

Now the trees and sky and ground were all ajumble, and she had no idea where the drop-off even was. She grasped wildly and ended up looping a tree stump with one leg.

On her back, the top half of her body acting like a pendulum, she swooped so that her head was pointing down the mountain. Except there was no mountain, and she was staring at the sky through the trees.

The jolt of pain in her leg made her cry out, but she squeezed with everything she had. The world was still tumbling, and it took a moment for her brain and eyes to catch up with each other. Gasping for breath, little lights swimming in front of her eyes, she wrapped her other leg around the tree stump, hugging it for dear life. The top half of her was dangling over the drop-off.

She squeezed her eyes closed and counted to five, trying to collect herself and think of a plan, realizing that her legs couldn't hold her like this forever.

When she reopened her eyes, she saw hands reaching for her.

"Grab on," Patrick said.

She shook her head. "I could pull you down."

"You won't. Grab on."

She hesitated, so he produced a rope out of nowhere. He looped it around the same tree that held her legs, then looped it around himself, tying a tight knot. He did it so quickly that she thought maybe she was imagining things.

He took off his gloves and tossed them to the side, then reached down again. "Now you can't pull me over. Grab on."

She reached for his hands, but he grabbed her wrists instead, and in one strong pull, she was up and sitting near the ledge, her arms and legs wrapped around the tree, her forehead pushed against it while she caught her breath.

"That was crazy." He, too, was breathing heavily. "Are you okay?"

She was holding the muscles so tightly, her legs felt seized into position. But somehow there was no pain.

"You saved my life," she said, her head still pressed to the tree trunk.

"I'm just glad I was here."

"I am, too," she said. "That was quick thinking."

"I considered thinking slowly, maybe drawing up some schematics," he said, "but you were, you know, hanging headfirst over a cliff. Fast seemed like the better choice."

She turned so she was facing him and chuckled. "I'm glad you weighed your options."

He pretended to brush off a sleeve. "Well, I am a rescuer, after all. And I'm glad you didn't fall. I have absolutely no idea where I am. I'd be up here so long, I'd probably miss lunch."

"Well, it's good to know where I stand in regards to lunch."

"Most important meal of the day." Again, he reached for her. She slowly unwound her legs. "Easy," he said. "Easy."

She was taking it easy, expecting the stabbing pain of something out of place to kick in any minute. But when she got to her feet, she was pleased to find that everything seemed okay. She bent and straightened her legs just to be sure.

Patrick seemed truly in awe. "You must be made of mountain stuff," he said.

"You wouldn't be the first person to say that." She turned and surveyed the view in front of them. "I don't usually lose my footing like that. Just goes to show that anyone can find themselves in need of rescue." She had a brief flashback of the couple she'd rescued the day before, and how she'd been so put off by their situation. Maybe she shouldn't have been so quick to judge. "Anyway, let's go down this drop the right way. I'll show you how to down-climb, but I'm thinking we've had enough excitement for a few minutes and should get out the ropes. Do you know how to set a belay?"

Patrick wasn't just quick on his feet; he was a quick learner. In no time, he had the basics of down-climbing and scrambled his way to the bottom of the drop-off without trouble. Erin was glad to be on flat ground again and was grateful for the gentle slope that would take them into the notch and to their destination.

They walked for about an hour before a tiny chapel first began to peek through the trees at them, like a child playing hide-and-seek. Erin had visited this chapel so many times before, she could have walked to it with her eyes closed. She'd often wondered who built it here, hidden between mountains, so shaded by trees you couldn't even see it from above, so small that a congregation of twenty would feel cramped inside. She was sure it had a history; she only wished she knew what it was.

She was also sure there was something about the chapel that made her feel safe and loved. Bigger than romantic love. The kind of love she'd felt on the hilltops in the holler. The love of God.

Sometimes she felt as if the chapel had been placed there just for her. A gift she was happy to receive.

She quickly glanced back at Patrick, but his goggles and gaiter concealed his reaction. She didn't know how he felt about magical chapels or bigger love or God's love...or love at all. Soon the chapel was right in front of them, its roof spattered with the snow that made it through the trees.

"Rest stop," she said before pulling open the door and going inside.

Patrick shuffled in behind her, and for a few moments, the only sounds were their breath and the grating of their shoes against the wood floor. It looked exactly the same as it had last time she was there.

She watched as Patrick studied the Stations of the Cross that had been painstakingly carved into the walls surrounding them, then went to a stained-glass window and put his hand against it. He gazed at the crucifix nailed above the small podium that served as an altar.

"Where did this place come from?" Patrick asked.

Erin shrugged. "I have no idea. I just stumbled on it one time during a hike, and as far as I know, I'm the only person who ever comes here. I've never seen any other footprints or people. It's like my own personal chapel."

From far away, Erin heard a scream. It was long and drawn out, a girl's screech, followed by what sounded like loud sobbing.

"Did you hear that?"

Patrick cocked his head. "Hear what?"

They were silent for a moment, listening. But the sound had gone away, and now Erin wondered if she'd imagined it.

"Must have been the wind," she said. "Never mind." But she was definitely keeping her ears perked in case she heard the sound again.

Patrick sat on one of the short wooden pews. "It's peaceful here."

Erin sat next to him. She could feel the blood warming in her cheeks, making them tingle. "That's why I like it here. I can think, pray...apologize."

He turned to her. "Apologize?"

She dipped her face down to her lap. She hadn't meant for that to pop out. "I just meant, you know, everybody has things they're sorry for. Saying you're sorry doesn't really undo everything. Sometimes you have to have bigger ears listening. I mean...forget I said that. I shouldn't have said *apologize*."

"No, no, I get it." The chapel brought out a somber side of Patrick that she hadn't seen yet. "You're right. We all have things to apologize for. Sometimes really big things."

She studied him, waiting for more, but he didn't offer it. Instead, he twined his hands together and bowed his head. She did the same.

Hi, God, she prayed. *I just wanted to check in here one last time before I go. Thank You for leading me to this little chapel. It's brought me so much peace. But I'm learning I can't find the peace I truly need while I'm still here. All I think about is what happened, and I can't keep doing that to myself. I know You understand. I know You put this chapel here for a purpose, and that it's served that purpose. Thank You.*

When she looked up, she was surprised to see Patrick staring directly at her. All the playfulness he usually carried around was gone, replaced with concern.

"You okay?" he asked.

Only then did she feel the wetness on her cheeks. Quickly, she swiped away the tears. "I'm fine. Just saying goodbye. It's hard."

"Do you always cry when you leave this place?"

"Not goodbye to this chapel. *Goodbye*, goodbye." She didn't know why she was telling him this.

His eyes grew wide. "You're not, like, sick or something…?"

She chuckled and sniffed, feeling silly for being so emotional. She was explaining a lot more than she'd intended. She took a deep breath. The cat was already out of the bag. There was no putting it back in now. She might as well come clean. "I'm leaving Gorham.

I'm leaving this mountain. Probably leaving climbing altogether."

"So is PARR...shutting down?"

"No. Someone else will take it over. Maybe Rebbie, now that I think about it. She's been with it since the beginning. She knows the ins and outs better than I do. I'm just the mountain jockey. She's the brains."

He nodded. "I got the impression she was a force to be reckoned with. But you're leaving? Why?"

"It's a long story." Erin reached out toward him. "Don't say anything to Rebbie, okay? Don't say anything to anyone. You're the first person I've told, other than my neighbor."

He rocked back a little. "Why me?"

"I don't know," Erin said honestly. "I met with a Realtor this morning, so it's on my mind. And we're here, and Tuckerman Ravine is right over that way. The closer I get to it, the more certain I become that I need to never see it again."

"What's up with Tuckerman Ravine? Do I need to know something about it? Is it dangerous?"

For an entire year, Erin had felt glued shut. Not just her mouth, not just the tears in her eyes, not just her gut or her throat or her thoughts. Her entire soul felt jammed closed, unable to reckon with everything that had happened. But now, her last time in this tiny chapel, so close to the ravine, she felt the glue weakening, her resolve breaking. Her breath hitched, but she kept the sob at bay.

"Last year, something happened. My climbing partner, Jason..." Suddenly, she didn't know how to tell the story. Were there actual words that could describe the horror and pain? It didn't seem like words would be enough. "He, um…he got called up to Tuckerman Ravine. It's not unusual. People get stuck on Tucks all the time. It's really tough, and everyone thinks they're better at hiking and skiing than they are. Anyway, I had gone home, and I laid down for just a minute. One minute. I fell asleep."

Patrick's face went soft, as if he knew what was about to come. Erin was shaking, trying to hold herself together, while knowing she was going to let it out. She just wasn't sure why she was letting it out now. To Patrick. A man she barely knew. She definitely wasn't going to tell him *everything* that happened that day. Just the basics.

"Three college kids got stuck. They were partying and weren't prepared for the trek. I missed the call, so Jason went without me. And…" She clasped her hands together and shook her head sorrowfully.

"He fell?"

"Snow arch," she said. "Collapsed on them. Killed them all."

"Oh, my."

"Yeah. I woke up from my nap to Rebbie pounding on my front door, hysterical. I thought she'd never forgive me for what I'd done, and I wouldn't blame her. But it turns out, I can't forgive myself. Jason was my best friend. He's gone, and it's my fault."

"It's not your fault," Patrick said, placing a hand over hers. Even through their gloves, she could feel a connection.

She closed her eyes and shook her head. "You don't understand."

"Don't be so sure of that," he said with an edge of regret that was very familiar to Erin.

"What do you mean?"

He gave her a long look, as if he was going to say something. It was the same serious look she thought she'd seen pass over his face during the interview, and just as quickly, it was gone. But he shook his head, as if shaking away a thought. "I don't think you owe anyone an apology for something you couldn't control."

"But I do." If only he knew.

"No." He regarded her intensely. "You don't. I believe that. I have to."

Erin frowned. He was trying to tell her something, she was sure of it. "Did you...?"

There was the scream again. Actually, two of them. Erin could have sworn she heard the word *help* on the tail end. But just as quickly, the sound was gone. And Patrick didn't appear to have heard anything.

A gale of wind rattled the window behind them and they both turned. It hadn't seemed like they'd been in the chapel for very long, but the sky was brightening with incoming snow, and it wouldn't have been the first time Erin had lost track of time in here.

Patrick stood. "I should have brought a sail. We'd be to the top in no time," he quipped.

Just like that, the spell between them was broken, the seriousness gone. It was as if Erin had never said a word about Jason—in fact, she was starting to wonder if she actually had. Maybe she'd only said those things in her head, as her mind wandered after her prayer. Either way, it was probably best to let it go and get back to business.

"We should start moving," she said. "Head back to the trail."

They double-checked their gear and loaded up. Patrick caught Erin's arm just as she reached for the door. "Thanks for sharing with me," he said.

She nodded, but found she had no response. "You're welcome" seemed entirely wrong. "My pleasure" was a complete lie. "No problem" was too glib. She pulled open the door and stepped back onto the snow in silence.

She found herself hiking at a fast pace and could hear Patrick's heavy breathing behind her. She slowed but stayed ahead of him, unsure how to face him again after laying her soul so bare. She concentrated on the ever-changing and precarious landscape beneath her feet and listened for more screams, eventually convincing herself it was only the wind in the trees that she'd heard in the first place.

They were nearing the trail when she noticed they were suddenly back in line with the footprints they'd seen down at the beginning of the trailhead. Whoever was hiking was still at it, or at least had been when they'd reached this point on the mountain.

The prints led in another direction, which meant they'd also gone off-trail. Erin felt unease creep up her spine. Had they gone off for a reason, or had they gotten lost? Maybe the altitude and the cold disoriented them. It had certainly happened before and could have deadly consequences. Regardless, she kept her eyes rooted to the footsteps, looking for any sign of the people who'd made them. Maybe she had heard a scream, after all.

It was another forty minutes before she found it. The indentations led to a cluster of pines.

"Huh," she said aloud, turning slightly to follow them.

"What?" Patrick asked. In her concentration, she'd almost forgotten he was with her.

She pointed to the ground. "These. We've been following them for quite a while. They're just...unusual." She plucked her walkie-talkie off her belt and fiddled with the volume. It was turned up, so it was unlikely she'd missed a distress call. Unless, of course, the device wasn't working. She pressed the button on the side. "Rebbie? It's Erin."

"Showing off the chapel, I see," Rebbie responded. It wasn't unusual for Rebbie to monitor Erin's whereabouts on the GPS, just in case. She hadn't ever been up here, but Erin had described it to her enough times that she often claimed she could draw a picture of it if asked.

"I didn't miss a call from you, did I?"

"Nope. Been quiet here. Why?"

"We just ran across some footprints. We're pretty far off-trail, so I thought maybe there was a chance someone was wandering."

"If they are, they aren't asking for help. Not all those who wander are lost, boss."

Erin chuckled. "Thank you, J. R. R. Tolkien."

"Bet you didn't know one of those *R*'s stood for Rebbie, did you?"

"I learn something new every day with you, that's for sure."

"Don't worry, boss. I'll keep my ears open. If I

hear anything about wanderers on the Adams, you'll be the first to know."

"Thanks."

"You're welcome, my precious."

Erin put the walkie-talkie back on her belt. Rebbie was a hoot, but Erin still couldn't take her eyes off the prints. There was just something about them that nagged at her.

"I'd still kind of like to see where they go, just in case," she said.

"In case the people at the other end of them need help and can't call for it," Patrick said.

"Exactly." She paused. "You're sort of a natural at this."

But when they pushed their way into the cluster of pines, they didn't find people. Instead, they found what seemed to be a bare spot, as if something had kept the snow from gathering on the ground. Around the bare spot, there was a jumble of footprints going in all different directions. Erin scanned the area.

"Ah," she said and pointed.

Patrick studied where she was indicating. "Skis?"

She shook her head. "They're going uphill. And you can see the tread in the center. Snowmobile tracks. Very weird."

"It wouldn't be my first pick of places to take a snowmobile, but it is a snowy mountain. What makes this weird?"

"Well, they obviously had it parked here, but why? Why park so far into the trees?"

"Maybe to get down faster?"

"Maybe," Erin agreed, but again, the snowmobile

tracks went uphill, not down. Of course, it was possible that its passengers only went uphill to get to a more open spot before heading down. A little extra *oomph* for that last stretch. "But I also don't see any tracks leading here, other than footprints."

"Which means they had parked here for a while," he said.

"Exactly."

"Yeah, that is interesting. Maybe it was abandoned, and they just stumbled upon it? Or maybe it broke down on them and it just took a few days for them to get back up here with the parts to fix it?"

"Two snowmobiles broke down at the exact same time?"

"Or one did, so they abandoned both because they knew they were coming back."

Erin supposed these things were possible, but she couldn't shake her intuition that something weird was happening with these tracks.

"Let's follow them a little," she said.

"It's kind of the opposite way of Grouper Giggles, though. Will we be able to find our way back?"

She turned, pulling down her goggles so she could see him better. "I know this mountain like the back of my hand. We'll be fine." But that nagging voice inside her head just wouldn't stop.

So did Jason. And look what happened.

It was true. Sometimes even something you knew well could still surprise you.

Plus, there was that scream.

Chapter Six

Nobody knew this mountain better than Erin. And not just the mountain they were currently on—Patrick wasn't even sure which one they were currently on—but the entire range. She'd spent a lot of time up here. He wondered if there would come a day when he would be able to say he'd spent as much time on the mountain as Erin Hadaway. Probably not. She was one of a kind.

In fact, she was so intriguing, he was finding that he wanted to know more and more about her. From what he'd already ascertained, she was like no other woman he'd ever met—fiercely independent but deeply connected, quick-witted, kind, shy, funny and filled with faith—and the fact that he was comparing her to other women startled him a little. No doubt, he was developing feelings for her that went beyond trainer and student. He was imagining spending time with her off the mountain. The idea of sharing a romantic dinner with her thrilled him.

Patrick found he was so winded trying to keep up

with her that he didn't even have time to think about his sister. He'd been afraid he would be able to think of nothing else. There were some benefits to spur-of-the-moment decisions like learning to do mountain rescue when you weren't really all that versed in climbing to begin with.

But his sister was up here with him. He could hear her in the wind that whistled through the trees, see her in the beams of sunshine that occasionally pushed their way through the clouds and diffused themselves through clustered leaves. The result was always jarring to him, and he worked hard to keep it at bay. Small talk was good. He could do small talk. *Let's chat about business. Real estate, yes, yes, how engaging.* And golf meetings—had he really mentioned something so boring? Erin must think him an intolerable bore. But at least it kept his mind busy.

Now they were following a set of snowmobile tracks. He didn't exactly understand why, but he would have to admit he found it kind of exciting. Or at least interesting. Like they were being mountain detectives. Erin was definitely thinking something about these tracks, and now he wanted to know exactly what. Even if he would be very, very sore tomorrow from all this investigating.

He kept his eyes on the ground, careful not to take a misstep from fatigue. The good part of being off-trail was that there seemed to be wider ground to cover. The bad news was that it was uneven ground, and the slope was steep enough that he feared he might go skidding all the way back to the parking lot if he stepped wrong.

He heard Erin gasp. "I had no idea," she mumbled. She pulled up short, and he nearly stumbled into her back.

Up ahead, where the notch had opened into a basin, was a cabin—one that looked as if it had spent years being digested by the mountain. The wood was weathered and cracked, bleached by the sun, and the gutters were dripping with dead vegetation and bird nests. Several shingles were missing entirely, giving the roof the look of a child's first carved jack-o'-lantern.

All around the cabin were cliffs and ridges, a tree line on one side and open ravine on the other. No matter if you were a climber, a snowmobiler or a skier, this spot had something for you.

The snowmobile tracks led right up to the front door. But, curiously, there was no snowmobile.

"I had no idea this was even here," Erin said. "I can't believe I've never seen it before. Maybe they're parked around back."

"Maybe they live here," Patrick said, feeling very uneasy about stalking whoever had been on these snowmobiles.

She shook her head. "I don't think so. Look how run-down the place is. I'll bet nobody has lived in it for fifty years. Maybe more. It may be that someone got lost and went into the cabin for shelter. We should make sure nobody is in distress."

But Patrick wasn't sure if they'd fully explored the possibility that the cabin was the snowmobile owner's home, and they were about to be greeted by someone who might be very unhappy to have intruders trudging around their property. After all, someone who lived all the way out here obviously didn't want to be bothered by other people.

Or whoever lives here might be really lonely and will ply us with gallons and gallons of hot coffee and a roaring fire. That would be okay.

But when they got to the back of the cabin, there was no snowmobile to be found. Instead, there were more tracks, this time leading uphill on the other side, just as he'd suspected.

He and Erin stood side by side at the back door, staring at the retreating tracks. His breath was making his gaiter moist and irritating. He lowered it for some relief.

"Maybe they stopped in to warm up and then took the fast way down," he said.

"Maybe," Erin replied. She pulled down her gaiter as well and pushed her goggles up to the top of her head. He followed suit. "But don't you think it's weird that we haven't heard anything? Like a motor? These tracks look really fresh and it's just…silent. Listen."

All Patrick could hear was the wind, and the occasional shrill call of a very loud bird.

Or. Wait. Was that…? That was no bird.

Erin froze at the same exact moment he had this realization. "Did you hear that?"

They stilled even more than before, both of them barely breathing, and strained to listen through the noise of nature.

There it was. Again. A warble of some kind. Or a…

"A cry?" Erin asked. "Does that sound like a girl crying to you? I knew I heard something before."

It did sound like a girl crying, and now he could

tell that it was coming from behind him. From inside the cabin. Without another word, they both jumped into action. Erin went straight for the back door and knocked, pounding hard with the heel of her fist.

"Hello?" she called. "Is anyone home? Hello!"

Patrick went the opposite direction, standing tall to peer through grimy windows, using his sleeve to wipe away some of the worst of the dirt so he could see inside.

The interior of the cabin looked just as dilapidated as the exterior, with the added bonus of discarded garbage accumulated in the corners. He saw a grubby kitchen, the cabinets flung open to expose rusted pots and pans, then moved to a window into a filthy bedroom, dominated by a mattress riddled with holes. The dust inside was so thick, he could see footprints in it, just like in the snow outside. And they looked fresh.

"Hello! Hello!" Erin had moved to the front door, pounding and calling.

He peered in each and every window—second bedroom, different view of the kitchen—until he got to a corner window near the back, a tiny submarine-type circle that he almost overlooked. He peered inside, his breath fogging the glass, forcing him to wipe it away and try again.

Inside, he saw the source of the faint cries. A girl, dirty and shivering, was tied to an old, unused woodstove. She was crying and calling for help. When she saw Patrick's face in the window, she cowered back into the corner between the stove and the wall, sobbing harder. She had blond hair and giant blue eyes that were tired and red-rimmed, and she was wearing what looked like pajamas.

He backed away from the window, thinking. He knew this girl. Not *knew* knew, but had definitely seen her face before. He just couldn't place where.

"Erin!" he called. "Erin! She's back here!"

Erin came running around the cabin toward him. Somewhere along the way she'd lost track of her goggles. Her nose was already beet-red from the wind. He nodded his head toward the window, and Erin immediately raced for it. She stood on her tiptoes to peer through. Instantly, the girl's cries ratcheted up a notch.

"Oh, no," Erin said. "How is...?" She turned to Patrick, seemingly trying to work something out in her head, as if what she was seeing through the window did not compute with real life. And it didn't. To Patrick, it looked like something you would see in a movie. Young girl chained up, crying, needing rescue. Kidnapped.

Kidnapped!

That was it! He realized where he'd seen that girl's face. He leaned in and took another look through the window to make sure. But he was already sure.

"That's Kerrington," he said. "Kerrington Hadley. She's from the island."

"The island?"

"New Castle. She was kidnapped—maybe three days ago? It's been all over the news. My dad and her dad know each other, so my family's circle of friends has been worried sick about it. Her kidnapper left a ransom note on her pillow, and the FBI are waiting to hear more from them. They definitely think she's still on the island, but they have no leads."

"They're not looking for her here," Erin said.

"No way."

"We have to get in there and help her."

But Patrick was already a step ahead of her, racing for the back door. He kicked over a couple of rocks, hoping maybe there would be a key hidden somewhere, before he remembered this wasn't someone's home, and probably hadn't been for decades.

So the good news was, nobody would be mad if he broke the doorjamb.

He lowered his shoulder and rammed into the door—once, twice—and then with a crack of wood, he was in. Kerrington's cries got louder and more desperate as Patrick and Erin burst into the cabin.

Erin got to her first, immediately dropping to her knees and inspecting the rope around her ankles.

"Who did this?" she asked. The girl was too panicked to answer. "How many are there?"

"T-two," the girl answered, her teeth chattering, although Patrick wasn't sure if they were chattering with cold or fear or pure adrenaline. His own teeth felt itchy.

"Men or women?" Erin asked.

"Men," the girl answered.

"Are you hurt?"

The girl squeezed her eyes closed and sobbed, nodded, shook her head, nodded again. Patrick had the sense that her most damaging wounds were on the inside.

"Can you walk?" Erin asked.

"I…think so," the girl answered. "I can't stand up, though, because of this stove." Patrick noted that she was only wearing a pair of thick socks on her feet. With the combination of cold and the tightness of the rope wrapped around her ankles, he imagined her feet were completely numb. Walking might take a minute.

"We've got to get you out of these ropes," Erin said. She examined the knot, then turned to Patrick. "Our pickaxes." He realized they'd both lain them against the cabin when they'd heard the cries.

He turned and ran back out, and that was when he heard a whine. He paused, lifted his head, pricked his ears. It was more of a buzzing sound—the hum of a couple motors approaching. He left the axes and ran back inside the cabin. Erin looked up at him expectantly as she continued to pluck and pull at the rope.

"The axes?" she asked.

He shook his head. "Snowmobiles. They're coming."

"No, no, no," the girl whined. Erin had gotten nowhere in freeing her.

"Are they close?" Erin asked.

"Close enough," Patrick said. "And getting closer."

Erin stood, heading for the window at the front of the cabin to check out the downhill side of the mountain.

"No!" Kerrington shrieked. "Please! No! Don't leave me here."

Patrick reached down and gave a few hearty yanks on the rope. It was tight. There was no way they would even be able to cut through it with the pickaxe before the snowmobiles reached the cabin. He could see now that Kerrington's wrists were raw and bleeding where she'd tried to pull free. Even her ankles appeared to be swollen around the binding.

The poor kid had really tried to get away.

"They want money," Kerrington said. "My dad has it. Bill Hadley. Call him—555-824-8676." Patrick could feel the desperation rolling off her. "Please. Call my dad. Please."

"Okay," he said. "We're going to help you. We are."

"They want money," she repeated, as if he hadn't ever said a word. "They have a gun. Please."

Now Patrick could hear the buzz of the snowmobiles from inside the cabin as well. They were getting really close.

"Did you say they have a gun?" Erin asked, lunging to the floor next to Patrick and pulling at the rope with him. Without saying a word, they began tugging in unison. Erin was incredibly strong, but still not a creak or a budge.

The girl nodded and paused as she finally heard the snowmobiles approaching again. Patrick could see her face slowly slacken with realization, and then she began pulling wildly, thrashing against the stove and creating new cuts in her bound ankles. She tried to stand, failed and fell to the floor.

"Kerrington—Kerrington…you have to let us…" Erin was trying to stop her, to still her, but it was no use. Kerrington flailed and knocked an elbow into Erin's jaw, hard. Erin made a soft *oof* sound and doubled over, clutching her jaw with one hand, but only momentarily, and then she was back in the fight.

Patrick was blown over by her strength.

But as the snowmobiles came into sight through the front window, where Erin had just been standing moments before, they all stopped moving and stared. Kerrington started to cry. "Don't leave me here."

"We need to go," Patrick said. Erin didn't move. He could tell she didn't want to go. He put both hands over Erin's, forcing her to look him in the eyes. "We can save her, but not if they shoot us on sight. We need to get out of here and make a plan."

She nodded, hesitantly at first, but with growing certainty. She stood and backed away from the girl on the floor.

Kerrington's cries turned into screeches.

"We'll be back," Erin said, her voice heavy with desperate emotion. "We're going to get someplace where we can safely call the police."

"Please! No! No! No!"

Patrick was momentarily taken back in time, to the terrified face of his sister, haloed by the fur around her jacket hood, her eyes dark pools reflecting moonlight back at him, a fine dusting of snow on one cheek. *Please don't go*, she'd pleaded. *Please, stay with me.*

But he hadn't. It was a move he'd regretted for his entire life.

"We will get you out of here, Kerrington," he said on his way out the door. "I promise."

Chapter Seven

Erin's heart broke as they left Kerrington. The girl's cries wrenched at her soul. But she knew Patrick was right. If they'd stayed, they could very well all be dead. They didn't even have their pickaxes inside the cabin to ward off the men. It was guns versus hands. Erin trusted her hands to get her out of many sticky situations, but gun battles weren't among them.

She barreled out of the cabin, grabbing her axes on the way, and prayed Patrick was following her. She thought she could hear his footsteps crunching on the snow and rock as they sped across the clearing and ducked into the trees. They steadily made their way to the denser part of the forest—where Erin would never recommend anyone unfamiliar with the mountain go. Even she could lose her way out here. It was hard to be rescued when your rescuer was lost. But they needed to get some distance between them and the kidnappers, and fast.

"They'll follow our prints," Patrick breathed behind her. He was closer than she'd thought.

He was right. Kerrington's scream and the broken back door would definitely tell the kidnappers that they'd had visitors. Erin and Patrick had left tracks in the snow, which would lead the kidnappers directly to them, just as they had followed tracks to the cabin. But the denser forest meant less snow. In some spots, the snow was stuck in the trees and never reached the ground at all. They just needed to get to a place where the kidnappers couldn't easily go.

"Follow me," Erin said.

She jutted even deeper into the forest and turned downhill, then looped around uphill again. What tracks they left would be in loops through trees that would be impossible to follow on the snowmobiles. If the kidnappers were on foot, they were at least on even playing field.

But she needed to be careful not to go too far away from the cabin. And she needed to get somewhere safe, where she could stop and call for help.

She saw a cliff face ahead. If there was anyplace she could go that other people couldn't, it was straight up.

Hooves, I tell you! The girl has hooves.

The question was, could Patrick handle this cliff quickly? This was going to be his moment to prove himself.

"Can you get up there?" she asked.

"I think so."

"Think?"

"I can. I'm sure."

She lingered a moment longer, trying to gauge whether or not she could trust Patrick. When he'd interviewed, she had definitely not trusted that he would know his way around a climb. She'd taken him up an incredibly difficult pass on a terribly windy day. She'd veered him off-mountain. She'd inserted herself into a kidnapping rescue without ever saying a word to him.

And he'd never once hesitated. He'd stuck with her this entire time, faithfully.

And he'd saved her life.

Maybe her first impression had been wrong.

She had to trust him. It was the only way to save Kerrington.

"Come on," she said and loped toward the cliff face. Once there, she slung her backpack onto the ground and unzipped it, quickly yanking out her jangling harness. He did the same. "We need to be fast and careful. Watch your footing, but trust your gut. Step where I've stepped. Move with me. I'll set belays as often as I can, but mostly we're going to solo it. When you get to anchors, if you can pull them, pull them. If these guys are going to follow us, I don't want to leave them any anchors. But if you can't easily pull them, leave them. We can't waste time. Got it?"

He nodded as he fumbled into his own harness, which had fewer carabiners and slings hanging off it, but still some. She had to give him credit for preparedness, if nothing else.

Suited up, she took a moment to assess him. Everything looked in order. When their eyes met, she felt nerves roiling off him, but also confidence. And something else. Trust? Loyalty?

"You can do this," she said.

She hooked herself up and started climbing the cliff

face, feeling quickly for handholds. In the distance, she could hear men shouting.

She set a belay on the first spike she found, then tugged the slack line to let Patrick know she was ready for him. She prayed he knew enough to pick up on her message. Soon, she could tell by the slack building up in front of her that he did. He had good instincts. Something else she could add to the pros list.

As soon as he reached her, she took herself off the line and continued climbing. She'd never climbed this face before and struggled to find cracks for her fingers, ledges for her feet. This both encouraged and terrified her. She knew she could get up and doubted the kidnappers could follow…but she was scared Patrick wouldn't be able to follow, either.

Plus there was the wind. The gusts felt like hands against her shoulders, pushing her down and away. Her forearms strained and trembled as she gripped the rocks by her fingertips with everything she had. There was no time to think or be scared. There was only time to get away.

She set a spike in a crack, attached a belay and yanked the rope again. Once more, Patrick found his way to her. And either she was going crazy, or he was moving even faster.

"Chimney," she whispered, pointing to a crack in the cliff face that was just big enough for them to climb. She propped her back against one side of it and her feet against the other, inching up using the tension of her legs alone, one small step at a time. When she reached the top and looked back down, Patrick was already halfway up the chimney, his long legs bent against the cramped space, the backs of his arms pressed on either side of him to help hold his back against the wall. She wondered if he'd ever chimney-climbed before. For some reason she doubted it, but you would never know that by watching him now.

She found a spot for another anchor, and as soon as he reached the top of the chimney, she found cracks and scrambled out of his way. There were still a good thirty feet to go.

Erin steadily worked her way up the cliff, stopping to let Patrick catch up, then moving upward again. It seemed like hours but was only minutes before she found herself breaching the top of a ledge. She scrambled to her knees and leaned over the side, watching Patrick make his way up the last few feet. She grabbed the back of his jacket and yanked him over the top, and together they worked to bring up the rope. There was still plenty of cliff above them, but this seemed like a good spot to rest and assess.

"They're coming after us," she whispered.

He nodded.

"I don't think they know where we are."

He shook his head. "I can still hear her, though."

Erin hadn't noticed it, but now that he said it, she, too, could hear Kerrington's cries again. The sound pulled at her gut. She felt abysmal leaving the girl there with those men.

"Come on," she whispered. "Maybe we can see them."

They both wriggled out of their harnesses and shoved them into their packs. While she was in hers, Erin pulled out her radio and clipped it back to her belt, but didn't dare turn it on for fear that it would squawk and give away their position.

They crept toward the side of the cliff that looked over the cabin and inched toward the ledge, dropping to a crouch the closer they got. All Erin could hear was her heart pounding in her ears, the whoosh of fear that the men would do something to the girl now that they knew they'd been found.

Dear God. Please let them come after us and leave her alone. Or maybe just have them go away entirely? I'll take care of getting her down.

They had to maneuver a bit to see the cabin, and now they were perched on a much smaller ledge, so close their shoulders were touching, their bodies expanding and contracting in unison as they breathed in sync. They watched as the two men burst in and out of the cabin, then stared up and down the mountain, searching for them.

There was a bit of an overhang above them and the rock was bare. She gestured for Patrick to get down and they both did, nearly lying on their stomachs while they watched the scene below. There were two men— one older and one younger. Bits and pieces of conversation rode the wind up to their ears.

"...had to have gone back down..."

"...too windy...nobody could get up the mountain in this..."

"...the woods..."

"...how was I supposed to..."

"...someone knows she's here now...if they went down..."

"...cops..."

And then, loud and clear… "We can't kill her as long as they're running around out there."

Erin and Patrick made startled eye contact.

"Just focus on the fact that they won't kill her," Patrick said.

"Yes, but if they kill us—"

"They won't if we keep away from them."

If, Erin thought. If she hadn't fallen asleep when Jason needed help. If Jason had waited for someone to go up with him. If those college kids hadn't been up there in the first place. If, if, if. A whole lot of horrible things can happen on the back of an *if*.

They watched the two men argue and then saw them notice the footprints leading into the woods. They followed Erin and Patrick's steps for several yards, argued some more, and then one of them stormed inside. The other pulled a key out of his pocket while stomping through the snow behind his accomplice. But instead of going inside, he jumped on one of the snowmobiles and brought it to life with a *whooom*.

Immediately, he aimed the snowmobile toward the trail they'd left behind, and once again Erin and Patrick made surprised eye contact. They'd known there was a possibility that the men would notice their prints, but they hadn't expected it to be so quickly.

"He's coming up here," Erin said.

"No, he's going into the woods," Patrick said.

"Which is exactly where we went."

"He'll lose our trail in there," Patrick said. "And besides, even if he knew we were up here, what makes you think he could get up here? He can't use a snowmobile to climb a cliff."

"Look around you," she said, gesturing to the scenery below. "Not only has he managed to get up here so far, but he's managed to bring an unwilling girl with him without leaving a trace. The police are looking for her a hundred miles from here. Whatever we do, we should not underestimate these men."

"The police," Patrick said, gesturing toward her belt. "You can call out now while the engine is running. He won't hear us."

"Good idea." Erin turned on the walkie-talkie and brought it to her mouth. "Rebbie, it's Erin, do you copy?"

There was a beat just long enough to make Erin grow taut with worry. If they didn't have Rebbie…

"What's up, Superwoman?"

"I need your help."

Another pause, then, "Aha! Decide he's the love of your life, after all?"

Erin was too worried to be embarrassed and too frightened to laugh. Just once, she wished Rebbie could be serious.

"No. We have a situation up here. I need you to call the police."

"Police?" Just like that, Rebbie was as serious as could be. "What's going on?"

"We have found a girl up here. Her name is Kerrington…" She glanced at Patrick.

"Hadley," he said.

"Kerrington Hadley," she repeated.

"So you did find someone at the other end of the mystery prints?"

"Yes. She's in distress, maybe hurt. She'll definitely need help getting down the mountain."

There was another pause, long enough that Erin checked to make sure her battery hadn't died in mid-conversation.

"O-o-k-kay," Rebbie said slowly. "Why can't you get her down the mountain? What happened?"

"She's been kidnapped," Erin said. "A few days ago, from New Castle. And her kidnappers know we're up here. We're kind of…trapped. They're looking for us. And they have a gun."

"What?! Okay. Okay, okay, um. Let me call Sheriff Grimes. Hang on."

Erin took a steadying breath. Rebbie was a whiz at her job. And it definitely helped that Sheriff Grimes was friends with Rebbie's father and had known her since she was a baby. He would do anything to help her. Besides, Grimes had made it clear many times over how much he appreciated PARR and Erin's work.

The radio came back to life. "Erin? You there?"

"I'm here."

"Bad news. The wind."

Erin already knew. Helicopters couldn't fly in high winds. That was what made rescues on windy days particularly dangerous and important—it was up to Erin and her team to get people down, because there was no other choice than doing it on foot. Erin knew, just by feel, that Tommy wouldn't go up in this wind. The sheriff's office was no different. It was physics. You couldn't argue with physics, no matter how much you'd like to.

"He's looking into getting a team up there on a snowmobile."

"But they'll hear that coming from a mile away," Erin said.

"Exactly. They don't want to give these guys any reason to…you know…"

"Kill the girl," Erin said. "Or us."

"Right. They're going to get in touch with the FBI to talk about options. It might take a minute."

"So what does Grimes want us to do?" Erin asked.

"Come down…?" Rebbie said, her voice small and tentative.

Patrick, who'd been watching over the cliff, turned and made eye contact with Erin. She knew exactly what he was thinking without him saying a word. And she knew they were on the same page.

Erin brought the walkie-talkie to her lips. "No way. I can't do that. I'm not going to leave that girl up here alone."

There was a pause. "I knew you'd say that. So did Grimes. Maybe send Patrick down, though? Since he's not fully trained?"

Erin glanced at Patrick again. They'd made a promise to come back for Kerrington, and Erin knew Patrick had meant that promise. He wouldn't go down the mountain any sooner than she would.

"His instincts are good," she said. "I need him up here." To her surprise, she found the last part to be true.

"If you're sure."

"I'm sure. Just tell Grimes the sooner, the better."

"He's working on it as fast as he can. Hang tight."

"Okay, and Rebbie?"

"Yeah?"

"Don't reach out to me. I might be in a situation where I need to be quiet. I'll reach out to you. Assume no news is good news."

"Understood. I hate that, but I get it. Just be safe, Erin. I don't want anything to happen to you."

There was a wobble behind Rebbie's words that told Erin she was close to tears. Rebbie was generally unshakable. Erin had only seen her cry once—when Tommy had finally brought Jason's body down from the Tuckerman Ravine.

Erin didn't want to think about Jason right now. She didn't want to think about how she could possibly let down Kerrington the same way she'd let him down. She had to come through for the girl.

There was no other option.

"Nothing will happen to me. You have my word," she said and quickly turned off the radio, before she could think about how sometimes what happened to you had nothing to do with your word.

Sometimes situations were simply out of your control, and you just had to do your best to hang on.

Chapter Eight

Patrick had never free-climbed like that before. It was probably good that he didn't have time to think, but just kept putting one foot in front of the other, taking up slack, hooking here, sliding there, continuing to move. Trying not to think about the gun behind him.

He may have actually been a little surprised to make it to the top, but he knew failure wasn't an option. It wasn't about embarrassment or saving face, it was about not dying. It was about not letting down Erin.

And not letting down Kerrington.

If he'd fallen or gotten injured, what might have happened to them? He wasn't sure.

He was glad not to find out.

They'd found a ledge with a pretty good view of the cabin. He didn't want to take his eyes off it. He would look away when the police arrived. *If* the police arrived. Which, from the sound of things, was a big *if*, and probably a long time from now.

Erin finished her conversation with Rebbie and stuffed the walkie-talkie back into her bag.

He tore his eyes away from the cabin. "So now what?"

Erin took a breath and let it out with a whoosh. "So now we're on our own. At least until the wind lets up and the police can get here."

The snowmobile stopped and they both leaned over the ledge, searching. Finally, they saw the man who'd been on it. He'd ditched the vehicle and was walking through the woods now, coming ever closer to the cliff. He stopped, scratched his head, looked around. When he craned his neck to look up, they both edged backward, pressing themselves against the rock. Patrick held his breath. He could hear his heart beating in his temples, and his throat suddenly felt parched. They waited a moment and then edged forward again. The man had turned and gone in a different direction, allowing them to breathe.

"We need a plan," Patrick whispered. "One of us needs to make sure they don't take her down the mountain."

Erin's eyebrows shot up. "What does that mean— 'make sure they don't take her'? How do we do that? They've got a gun."

"I'll go down there and disable the snowmobiles so they're stuck here."

"No way. Too dangerous."

"If they take her, we won't have any idea where she's gone. They'll probably kill her."

"And what if they kill you?"

He paused. He hadn't really absorbed this possibility yet. He would be the first to admit, it was a huge risk. But he found himself thinking back to the sermon he'd felt had been spoken directly to him—the one that had brought him here in the first place.

"'Cast thy bread upon the waters, for thou shalt find it after many days,'" the pastor had said. "'Give a portion to seven, and also to eight, for thou knowest not what shall be upon the earth. If the clouds be full of rain, they empty themselves upon the earth, and if the tree fall toward the south, or toward the north, where the tree falleth, there it shall be.'"

Patrick, who was no stranger to Ecclesiastes, had continued in his head: *He that observeth the wind shall not sow, and he that regardeth the clouds shall not reap.*

He'd heard these words before, many times in his life, but he'd never really stopped to consider them. In that moment, when his future was at its bleakest, he truly understood them for the first time.

He was done withholding himself. Observing the winds and never deeming it safe to step outside. Regarding dark clouds and hiding from rain that had already fallen long ago.

"I would rather die here on this mountain than have to live with…" He faltered. Now was not the time to get into guilts of the past. Although Erin seemed to be filling in the rest of the sentence herself, and he could see the hurt on her face that he was possibly insinuating he would rather die on the mountain than be like her and lose someone else here.

If only she knew how much they had in common.

"I just don't want something terrible happening to her," he explained.

Erin searched his face. Whatever she saw there—or maybe what she saw inside herself—must have convinced her.

"I'll go with you," she said, then corrected herself before he could even open his mouth to argue. "Actually, no. I'll go up. I'll lead them—or at least him…" She gestured at the man, who was still wandering the woods looking for them, getting angrier and more vocal every second. "I'll lead him away from the cabin. Get him lost."

"Divide and conquer," Patrick said.

"Divide and conquer," she repeated. She grasped his hand and gave it a squeeze that he felt deep down in his soul. "You're sure about this?"

He squeezed back. "I have to do this."

"*We* have to do this," she said. "If you get into any trouble, yell. I'll go up as far as the tree line will go. But once I get past the tree line, up at the peaks, I'm out in the open. If he has a gun—"

"Too dangerous," Patrick interjected. "I agree."

"Can you get back down safely?" Erin asked as she checked the equipment on her belt.

The truth was, he would have felt way more comfortable trying to get down on a pair of skis. And it had been so long since he'd done that, he wasn't even sure if he would be comfortable with that anymore. But she had shown him how to down-climb earlier. It wasn't ideal. But he could do it.

"I'm good," he said. "I wanted to be a rescuer. I

didn't realize it would be this kind of rescue, but I said I was up for anything, right?"

Erin nodded, but he still sensed some worry in the air that wormed its way into his nerves. This wasn't an action movie, and it certainly wasn't part of his normal day in real estate development. He really had no experience to prepare him for this, and who did? There was a real gun; he couldn't ignore that. And two real men who'd already gone to great lengths to get what they wanted. He couldn't ignore that, either.

"Listen," he began, "if something happens to me, don't come trying to save me or anything. Just get yourself out."

"No way," Erin said. "We finish this together. That's what climbing partners do."

"This isn't a normal climbing situation. If I can't make it down, you have to cut me loose, get yourself safe and go for help."

"Cut you loose? I couldn't just leave—"

"You have to. For Kerrington."

She shook her head but didn't say anything more.

He stepped back into his harness, checked the equipment to make sure everything was good to go, then pointed to the left, indicating that he would travel as far toward the other side of the mountain as this ledge would let him go, then rappel down from there. Once he got down, he planned to make his way back through the woods until he got to the cabin, and hope that Erin was successful in luring the man up top. Erin nodded as she donned her own harness and strapped her pickaxe into its holster, making sure everything was tight and ready to go.

It was all or nothing now. Time to stop regarding the wind and push himself into it. Let it carry him away. Literally.

He put his head down and began scrambling over the smaller rocks and boulders, creeping higher while getting farther away from Erin.

He had just lost sight of her completely when he heard her voice echo through the quiet trees.

"If you want to catch me, you're going to have to work harder than that!"

Their plan was officially on.

Chapter Nine

As soon as Patrick walked away, Erin felt his absence. She didn't like it one bit. Just hours ago, if asked, she would have said she thought he could be wasting both of their times. She would have called him flippant. She would have brought up any number of accidents and near accidents that had happened over the years due to guys like Patrick.

She would have been wrong. Patrick could have insisted that they bail on Kerrington and just get back to base. He could have clung to her, claimed not to have enough training, flipped out and panicked—and rightfully so. She was trying very hard not to flip out and panic herself.

Erin had to give it to him—he was brave. And he wasn't doing it out of bravado or a misplaced yearning for adventure. She was almost sure of it. She thought he might be doing it for another, deeper reason he hadn't shared with her.

Perhaps she wasn't the only one carrying a heavy weight up this mountain.

She waited until she couldn't hear the clink of his harness over the wind anymore, then stood. Her legs shook and her heart felt as if it would skip right out of her mouth when she opened it.

Just focus on Kerrington, she thought. *If you're scared, just think of how terrified she is.*

She took a breath to steady herself, then waited until the man below appeared into her line of sight again.

"Hey!" she yelled, but the wind swept it away.

"Hey!" she called again, louder.

The man's head whipped around wildly as he tried to figure out which way the voice was coming from.

"Up here!"

His gaze snapped up, and the furious snarl on his face nearly made Erin stumble backward. He found her, and now she was questioning why she'd wanted him to follow her in the first place. Surely there had been other, safer options.

But what was done was done, and since when did safety and mountain rescue ever go together?

"If you want to catch me, you're going to have to work harder than that!" she yelled, hoping he couldn't hear her voice faltering.

She was filled with a sinking feeling as he took a moment to puzzle over the situation. She'd never thought about what she might do if he decided not to follow her. Would she have to come down and lead him on a chase down there? She could still probably outpace him, but the playing field would be literally and figuratively much more level.

Actually, he had a snowmobile and a gun, so he would have the definite advantage.

"I saw her!" Erin shouted. "I saw Kerrington. I know who she is, and I know she was kidnapped from her home." She saw the man's eyes dart over the cliff face. There was no going back now. She'd started this train rolling; now it was up to her to stay out of its way. "I know what you look like now, too. I'm sure the police will find that information very helpful. Actually…" She reached around and unzipped a side pocket of her backpack. Her cell phone was inside. She grabbed it, pulled up the photo app, pointed it at the man and snapped a photo. He brought up his hand to shield his face just a moment too late.

"Got you!" she said. "Now everyone will know exactly what you look like."

"You're dead!" the man yelled. Erin tensed her muscles, ready to spring back if he reached for his gun, but he never did.

Which probably meant he didn't have one, and the two men only had one gun between them. The other man was likely using it to defend the cabin from… her. This thought bolstered her. All she had to do was stay one step ahead of this man and she would be safe. And she was certain she could do that.

She only wished she could warn Patrick that the gun was right where he was headed. They were both going to have to rely on his instinct.

"You'll have to catch me to kill me!" she said, her voice losing some of its bravado. Her arms and legs suddenly felt weak. *Nerves,* she told herself. *It's just nerves. You can scramble this mountain all day.*

There was no bailing out now. The man had already started up. And, as she suspected, he looked experienced. Free-climbing without a line was risky, but he was clawing up the mountain as if he didn't have a care in the world. He was strong. And he was good.

But Erin was better. She had to be.

She turned in the opposite direction that Patrick had gone, taking her away from the cabin. She knew the mountain well enough to know that this was bringing her closer to the trail. Which would be good for her, but would also make things easier for the man. Still, she had to go there. The farther from Kerrington she got, the farther he got.

She hoisted herself up and over a few more rocks, until she reached more even ground, then she began running, looking over her shoulder only a few times to make sure the man hadn't made up the distance between them. She didn't like the way she was breathing—fast and hard and panicky.

As a child, she and her siblings had often played tag in the mountains. She was never tagged, always able to effortlessly bushwhack her way to safety while everyone else grunted and struggled to find a spot below. She tried to channel that child now. Find a calmness that would slow her breathing.

Finally, she saw the man pull himself over the lip of the cliff. She wanted nothing more than to hide, but knew she needed to let him see her so he would keep following and not double back to the cabin.

"You won't get away with it!" she called, in order to attract his attention.

They locked eyes, and then he came after her. Even

though there was still a good bit of distance between them, she felt terror fill her heart and lungs and limbs as she pushed through the brush, praying that she kept her footing.

The wind was in their faces now and drove into Erin's shoulders as she pressed forward. She felt as though she was running through shoulder-high mud. Her legs were getting tired. Her lungs felt frozen. The man, bigger than she was, didn't seem to be slowed by the wind at all. She watched as he closed the gap between them, his face set into a snarl. She could hear him tromping behind her now.

She feared she'd let him get too close.

He was going to catch her.

Chapter Ten

Patrick was trying, and struggling, to stay on alert as he made his way down the cliff and back toward the cabin. He was too aware of every scrape of his shoes against the rocks, and every gale of wind sounded like Erin or Kerrington calling for help. He was too vigilant that the handholds fit his palms perfectly. He was too conscious of everything around him, and even things he only imagined were around him, until he was questioning whether there were winter animals up here that could eat him if he wasn't careful.

Was this what it would always be like to be a rescuer? Surely, he was just on high alert.

The truth was, he had no idea how he managed to pull Erin up and over that ledge. He didn't even remember how he got to her. It all just seemed to happen, as if he was being guided by a force he couldn't exactly see.

He only wished he'd been visited by that same guiding force when he and his sister had been on the mountain.

Kerrington looked like his sister. That was part of why he remembered the girl's photo from the newspapers. Big blue eyes. Blond, slightly wavy hair. A mouth that turned up at the corners, as if she was always on the verge of telling the funniest joke. It was that same bemused half smile that led him to call his sister "Haha" instead of Hannah. He'd had a bad sense of déjà vu when he saw the news of Kerrington's kidnapping. Something about seeing that face on newsprint. It seemed like just yesterday there were grainy black-and-white photos of Hannah plastered everywhere.

Photos that were seared into his eyes and his brain and his conscience.

Photos that bore their way into his family and cleaved them apart, as easy as ripping the newspaper in half.

He wondered if his parents had also experienced being transported back in time when they saw Kerrington's face in the paper. Back to the worst headline he could imagine:

Daughter of Real Estate Mogul Dies in Tragic Ski Accident

"You did this, you know," his mother had said, the paper clenched in her fist, her voice thick with accusation and anger and something much, much deeper. He would have called it grief, but it seemed deeper than that, even. A grief she would never move on from.

"Linda, it was an accident," his father had said, but his words were small and plaintive. Patrick's father had, on the surface, understood what had happened the night Hannah died. He'd understood that it was a terrible error in thinking. He could understand and forgive, but he couldn't look Patrick in the eye ever again.

"It was negligent. It was avoidable. It was irresponsible," his mother had responded. Patrick had expected her to burst into tears once again, but the doctors had given her something to help dull the pain. As far as he could see, though, the pain was still as strong as ever; it was simply the response to the pain that got dulled. Like watching someone scream through the window of a soundproof room.

Or inside an isolation booth.

"Mom, I've told you, I never meant—" he'd begun.

"You left her," she said. And that was all she needed to say to end the conversation. He couldn't count how many conversations had been ended that way since the accident. In some ways, every conversation ended with it, because they never began in the first place, in the chasm that was his family.

What would his mom say when she found out he hadn't left Kerrington? He would be fooling himself if he said her approval wasn't in the back of his mind. Was he trying to prove something to himself, or to his mother? Or maybe to the mountain itself? Was he telling the mountain "You can't take from me again"?

He found a shallower slope and crept down it, eventually sitting on the ground and sliding on his backside. They called descending in this way glissading, he recalled from the studying he'd done after making his decision to join PARR. You had to be careful you didn't get out of control with it, though, or you could glissade your way right over a cliff. He kept his heels pointed toward the ground for an easy dig-in should he need to stop suddenly. The wind was at his back, pushing him faster and faster and faster.

Soon the cabin was in front of him. He stopped and ducked into a grove of trees and brush, then just watched. He'd never heard the snowmobile restart, so Erin must have had the searcher on the run. The thought made his heart ramp into gear. He wanted to go to her, to make sure she was protected. He wouldn't feel settled until he was sure Erin was all right. She was the most fearless person he'd ever seen, but fearlessness wouldn't save her from the destruction of a weapon, no matter who she was.

He watched the cabin. Inside, he could see the movement of shadows, like someone was in there pacing, watching the windows. He stayed as still as a stone, willing himself not to shiver as the wind whipped through him. They'd never discussed that they would likely be on this mountain after nightfall. He couldn't imagine how cold the wind would feel then.

Hopefully Erin will be okay in the night, he thought, *and we'll find our way to each other again in the morning.*

He thought he heard the occasional voice echoing over the mountain, but then realized it was probably just the wind screaming through trees or blowing over the mouth of a cave, or who knew what. Maybe some other hikers would be crazy enough to be on the mountain in this kind of weather, too. Undoubtedly, they existed. They were why PARR existed.

As he watched, the shadowy movements inside the

cabin seemed to slow and then stop. The windows became too dark to see through, and they seemed to have no light source inside. *How terrifying that must be for Kerrington*, he thought. *Alone, in the dark, with a monster.*

The sky darkened and evening was upon them. Patrick finally felt like he could move from his position. He scooted out of the brush and crept toward the cabin, trying to stay as low as he could and make as little noise as possible, although he was so cold, he almost felt as if he had no control of his limbs.

The snowmobile was parked in front of the cabin. If he came at it from the far side, he could duck behind it and hopefully not be seen. If he got caught, and if Kerrington was right about the gun, he would be a goner. He was sure of it. But he had to do this, anyway. There was no backing down.

One of the best things about living a privileged life was the toys. And he had many. Including three snowmobiles parked in one of the bays of his parents' six-car garage. They were old, had been rarely used, but they were very similar to the one he was crouching behind now.

Once upon a time, when they were a family of four and life was good, Patrick loved his snowmobiles. He spent a winter practically living on one. He took care of it like it was a baby.

He knew exactly what to do to disable this one.

He opened the side compartment, which held the tool he would need to take off the engine cover, and then he worked quickly, spinning the tool deftly despite the gloves on his hands and the numbness of his fingers. In just moments, he had the hood off and was pulling out the spark-plug remover tool. A quick loosening of the plug and it was done. He pulled the extra spark plugs out of their spaces and pocketed everything. He quickly screwed the hood back into place and added the tool to his pocket. They would have no idea why it wouldn't start. And they wouldn't be able to fix it.

Finished, he crept toward a window, filled with an urgent need to see if Kerrington was okay. Erin would want to know. She would expect him to have checked on her. But what would he do if he popped up to peer into one of these windows, only to see the face of the kidnapper right on the other side, staring back at him?

Patrick was no small man. He could hold his own in a fight if he had to. But just as Erin couldn't out-climb a gun, neither could he outpunch one.

So don't pop up, he told himself. *Be slow and subtle. Make the kidnapper wonder if he's seeing things.*

He pressed his back hard against the wall of the cabin and slowly rose to standing outside the window that looked in on the kitchen. He closed his eyes and swallowed, then eased one eye into the corner of the window. Nothing. Just the tiniest sliver of Kerrington's socked foot sticking out in the far background.

He lowered himself and crouch-walked around the cabin to the window where he'd first seen her. It was a high window and a small one. He felt much more confident looking into it.

Kerrington was in the same position she'd been in when they'd left her. No surprise there—she was tied into that position. But her head was down, chin tucked to her chest, and her hair was hanging over her face so he couldn't see her. He could only see what looked like blood down the front of her shirt.

Had that been there before? If it had, he hadn't noticed it.

Had they beaten her? Surely they hadn't killed her. If they had, why wouldn't they flee the mountain?

But still, he couldn't leave until he knew she was okay. Couldn't tear his eyes away from her until he saw that she was alive. He reached up and tapped the glass with his finger. She didn't budge. He tapped again. Nothing. The third time, her head snapped up and she blinked blearily at the window.

She was alive. Her lip was split and there was dried blood on her chin. One of her eyebrows looked thick with blood, too. So they *had* beaten her. But, praise the Lord, she was alive.

At first, they simply locked eyes, hers pouring out a world of heartbreak—so deep and real, he could feel it in his chest. In that moment, he had the mind to burst into the cabin and rip the entire stove out of the wall, if that was what he had to do.

But he knew that in order to save her, he needed to leave her. Ripping out the stove would do no good if her captor would only wake up, shoot him and then go after her. She wouldn't make it two steps.

When Kerrington finally recognized what she was seeing, she began to grunt and squirm again, tugging against her ropes, trying to get loose. He could hear her little mewling noises all the way outside.

And then he sensed more movement inside the cabin. Sure enough, her kidnapper barreled into view.

Patrick ducked, but that didn't stop him from hearing what happened next.

"How many times do we have to tell you to shut up?" the kidnapper yelled, followed by a thud. "I don't know if you're even worth four million."

Patrick clenched his fists and held his breath, trying to withhold his urge to just go inside and end this. *Erin is out there*, he told himself. *If you die, you leave this entirely up to her.*

When he was sure the kidnapper had gone back to wherever he'd come from, he stole another peek through the window.

Kerrington was in the same position she'd been in when he first looked inside. Only there were new droplets of blood on her shirt.

Filled with rage and a renewed energy to save her, he scurried away, back to the brush, where he could keep an eye on the cabin. He wished he knew where the other snowmobile was, and considered going to look for it. He wished he knew where Erin was, and if she was safe.

He balled himself up against the wind and watched the vast, starry sky. Alone and small, Patrick felt the weight of what they were up against. The adrenaline had worn off. The plan had been executed. And now it was time to just…wait. And pray.

God, if You could…just keep us all safe and alive. And show me the way to help Kerrington. To get her out of that cabin. To get us all off this mountain.

When Pastor Elmer had preached about accepting God's gifts by using and sharing them, Patrick had been sure the message had been just for him—get back on that mountain and conquer it. But now that he was here, he realized there was no conquering mountains. That was what made them mountains. It was what made them alluring. It was what made them both dangerous and thrilling at the same time. Pastor Elmer hadn't sent him here to climb a hill. He'd sent Patrick here to climb the mountain of guilt within himself. To set right what had gone wrong. And he wouldn't do that by freeing a kidnapped teenager.

He would do that by freeing himself.

Once again, Patrick caught his mind drifting to Erin. Her regrets seemed as endless as the sky above him. There was more to her than the obvious beauty—the taut muscles and the high, freckled cheekbones. There was something deep in her soul that reached out to his.

They weren't just on this mountain together. They were standing at the base of an internal mountain at the same time, too.

And he wouldn't be able to go all night without knowing she was okay.

Chapter Eleven

Erin was cold. And tired. Her forearms quaked as she pulled herself up over yet another ledge. Her legs didn't want to bear her weight when she got there. She felt as if she'd been over every inch of this mountain. And she wasn't even sure which mountain she was on anymore. As night fell, she started to lose her bearings. She only knew she'd passed over the trail several times and trusted that meant she hadn't veered far from it.

At least she could hope the man was as disoriented as she was. That he was wandering in unfamiliar territory, and that the night had made the forest look different to him, too. The last thing she wanted was for him to give up on her and go back to the cabin. Who knew what would happen then? Would he take Kerrington away? Would he kill her? She didn't want to think about it.

Whatever he planned to do, if he went at it with the same focus he'd gone after her, he had a good chance of succeeding. Part of her was surprised he hadn't already succeeded in capturing her.

The man had gotten far closer than she'd meant to let him get. He was fast and powerful and, yes, he could climb. She'd definitely underestimated his abilities, assuming he was a kidnapper first who had just happened to end up in a remote cabin in the notch of two of the hardest mountains in the country to climb.

How naive of her.

Twice, he'd gotten close enough to touch the back of her snowsuit. Twice, she'd tapped into reserves of strength and energy she didn't even know she had. Once, when she was certain she had no more juice to give, he'd reached out to grab her and then lost his footing. The tumble only took him a short way down the mountain, but it bought her enough time to stretch the distance between them again, thanking God the entire way for having the strength that she didn't.

The man had gotten up and continued to lurch after her as if there had never been any interruption at all. The fall had cost him. He was limping and panting. They made eye contact one last time, and then she finally lost him. She'd found the ledge, small but deep, and climbed up, pushing herself into the shadows.

She was not a night climber, and in fact hated it when she had to go up after dark, and usually avoided it if there wasn't a child involved and the conditions were mild enough that the stranded climber could make it through the night. She didn't feel as secure, even if her hands and feet knew right where to go all by themselves. And even though she had a headlamp, she feared that turning it on would lead the man right back to her. Because if she knew one thing for certain, it was that he was out there just waiting for her to show herself.

Her ears played tricks on her, the *shhh* of the trees making her jumpy. She watched their limbs bend with the wind, but still heard voices in the creaking and scratching of the wood. She'd been confident when she and Patrick had decided to part ways. They'd had no choice, really. But now, she was terrified and wished he was here with her. Or at least that she had some way of knowing he was okay.

Anything could be happening to him, and she wouldn't know it because all that surrounded her were these rocks and trees and that ever-blowing wind.

She couldn't sit here all night. Being sheltered meant being unaware.

Slowly, she pivoted her body and got her feet under her. Above this ledge, the trees started to thin. She was too close to the peak. There was nowhere to hide up there.

At the same time, if she could get over the mountain, maybe in the morning, she could lead the man to an even more unfamiliar area. Lost was not the same as arrested, but it also meant he was not in the cabin with the girl.

Erin shuffled to the side, where there was a slight gradation, and carefully climbed until she'd found her way back to the trail. It was on the exact opposite side of where she'd imagined it to be. Which meant she had been turned around—a feeling she hated.

Her gaiter had fallen down around her neck in her flight, so she pulled it into place and peered down the dark path. She quickly lost sight of the trail as it led into the woods and couldn't help feeling the hairs on the back of her neck stand up at the thought of the man being down there, where she couldn't see. She didn't sense any movement, and was afraid of moving herself.

Most of her wanted to just make a run for it. Get over the peak and down into the notch. Find a safe place to recuperate and rethink. Build a fire and get warm. Eat an energy bar and drink from her water bottle.

Save herself.

But there was that part of her that would never die—the part that told her she was put on this earth to save others, not herself. She had the hooves to prove it.

She took a deep, steadying breath and turned to head up the mountain.

And found herself face-to-face with the man who'd been chasing her.

Chapter Twelve

His eyes gleamed hatred in the dark. His face, scraped and blood seeping under one eye, was pulled into a scowl so fierce she felt swallowed by the wrinkles. His bare hands were tightened into fists at his sides. He swayed slightly forward, his breath heaving clouds of mist in her face.

Erin screamed.

She hadn't meant to. It was pulled out of her involuntarily.

And then cut off involuntarily when the man grabbed her. He was surprisingly quick for how tired he must have been.

But she was quick, too. She wrenched free of his grasp and darted off-trail, making raspy sounds that were half grunt, half sob as she ran. Every few steps, she whipped a quick glance over her shoulder, every time hoping he would have fallen behind or given up. But every few steps, he was closer.

She had to think fast. If she could get up to the peak, she could possibly move more freely, no longer having to dodge trees and brush. Of course, if he had the gun, he would probably stop running and end the chase—and end Erin—very quickly.

But going down would require too much care. Her legs were already shaky and her footing unsure in the night. She'd already fallen once today and somehow survived. She couldn't take the risk of falling.

No, she had to go up. She willed her feet to move faster, churning them up and up and up the mountain, her tight leg muscles groaning, her shoes slipping on rocks and snow. As she ran, she had an insane, fleeting thought—*that was the first time I've ever been tagged on a mountain.*

It was that break in concentration that caused her to trip. She fell, the sharp edge of a rock digging painfully through her snowsuit into her shin. She tried to quickly stand again, but gravity tugged and then pulled and then yanked. She fell again. And then went down a third time, this time landing flat on her belly. She threw her arms and legs wide, trying to catch herself as, for the second time that day, she began sliding.

The man launched himself at her, his body slamming against her, ramming a rock into her solar plexus and stealing her breath, flipping her over. Thankfully, his body weight on top of hers stopped the momentum. If only she could get away. She gasped and writhed, clutching and flailing at the man, while stars floated in the backs of her eyes, begging her to take a breath. When her lungs woke up and she breathed again, it came in huge gulps that distracted her from the blows she was taking, the man swatting at her face and her shoulders while grabbing for her throat.

This is it, she thought. *I'm going to die here.*

No, she heard in Jason's voice, as plainly as if he'd been standing next to her. *Fight. You have to fight.*

She lashed out wildly and the heel of her hand struck the man's temple, hard. The blow caused him to lose his grip the tiniest bit. Erin took advantage of the pause and flailed harder, all four limbs working with everything they had to get herself out of his grasp. But the movement jolted her, and they hit a steeper patch, which set them both rolling helplessly again.

Too much. Too much was going on all at once. She couldn't fight the man and the ground and gravity all at once. Erin Hadaway, known for her calm demeanor and quick, decisive action, froze. Which was the worst thing she could do.

Soon she found herself sliding and rolling even faster down the mountain, boulders digging into her back, her sides, her head glancing off rocks, and her shoulder banging painfully into the trunk of a tree. The man tumbled with her, their arms and legs and torsos smashing into each other. Erin felt dizzy as they fell faster and faster.

She had to stop this momentum or they would both die, either from falling off the mountain, or slamming into something that would break them. But they were already going so fast.

Pickaxe. She still had her pickaxe.

She forced her arm around to reach for the holster on her harness. With a yank, she pulled out the axe.

The man immediately grabbed at the axe, and for a moment she wished that she hadn't introduced a weapon into the fight. She was sure he would wrestle it away from her, and the next blow she felt would be her last.

But she knew what to do. She'd trained for this many times, and she'd already disappointed herself earlier. She just had to let that training kick in. If she could get the axe under her, she could stop this fall.

Sliding helplessly on her belly, Erin grabbed the head of the axe with one hand and, with her other, held on to the pick end with everything she had, her arm muscles screaming like they were being torn from her body under all the pressure.

Finally, she was able to tip the axe toward the ground just enough to drag against the ice and rock. It caught, nearly pulling out of her grip, but she hung on and pulled her knees up so her crampons didn't stick in the ice and break her ankles. She pressed her shoulder forward and ground to a stop.

The man continued to roll, fruitlessly grabbing at her, his hands slipping away. She panted as she watched him go, hoping he would keep going until he was no longer in sight, because she wasn't sure if she could even get back on her feet. She needed to assess if anything was broken—from the feel of things, everything was.

The man's head whipped from side to side as he looked for a way to break his slide. He quickly found one about twenty feet away from Erin, hooking one arm around a small tree trunk. He let out a sharp roar as his momentum was abruptly stopped. His fingers slipped off the bark and he did a sideways roll into the trunk of another tree.

He looked as dazed as Erin felt, but that lasted

for only a few moments before his anger took over again, even more intensified. Fury seemed to be giving this man an unending source of fuel that her fear couldn't match.

On her backside now, she churned the ground beneath her knees and feet, trying to gain enough footing to get up. But the pitch was too steep and she was too dazed. She ended up scraping the ground in place. The good news was her legs were still working, and it seemed nothing was broken, after all.

The man used the tree to anchor himself and pulled to standing with effort. Blood trickled from the tips of his raw and scraped fingers. He panted clouds of anger as he stepped toward her. He wasn't moving fast, but at least he was moving, and she was getting nowhere.

Stop panicking, Erin, she told herself. *Slow down and pay attention*.

But it was impossible to remain calm with the man approaching her.

Chapter Thirteen

Erin had a new respect for the people she saved. She understood now how fear of the worst changed everything. How fatigue sweet-talked your body into just giving in.

"You don't have to do this," she said. "You can stop the whole thing." She hated how her voice sounded so plaintive and weak.

"You had your chance to get off the mountain alive," the man said. "You didn't take it."

"I wanted to protect the girl."

"You stuck your nose where it didn't belong."

"Please—" Erin hated begging, but she didn't see another option. She was down to imploring, and in some ways it felt like she'd been imploring on this mountain since the day she missed Jason's call. And it never got much past *please*.

The man came faster. Her arms nearly spent, Erin flipped to her hands and knees, gave one last heave and was able to get her knees under her, and then her feet. She kept her legs bent to absorb imbalance, and breathed evenly to keep herself calm and thinking clearly. She plucked the axe out of the snow and slammed it down again, inching herself up to a more level space. This she knew—chip and pull, chip and pull, chip and pull.

She wasn't moving fast enough. He was coming and coming. She'd often marveled at how, in the movies, the bad guys always seemed to have endless supplies of energy while their victims were easily spent. She'd always found it implausible. But here it was, happening to her. He looked just as spent as she felt. He was beat up and bloody. And he was still coming.

It was the fear. Fear made you foggy and tired. Fear made you forget what you knew.

She wasn't going to outrun him. She had to reason with him. She held out her arms, as if to stop him. But she was too late. He grabbed her again, pulling at her arms, dragging her toward the cliff edge. She fought, pounding at his hands and arms and back and chest and face, but she was weakening, and the blows were making no difference. He was stronger; that was all there was to it.

"I won't tell anyone," she said, her words ragged and desperate. "If you let me go, I'll just leave." He continued pulling her, inching toward the edge of a cliff. She hated how high on the mountain they were because there seemed to be an unending number of ledges to choose from. She understood now exactly what he planned to do.

He planned to throw her over the cliff.

"I'll forget I ever saw you. And her. I'll take it to my…" She'd been about to say "grave," but that seemed a little too on-the-nose at the moment. Instead, she concentrated on wedging her heel against a boulder so she could pull back against him. If he was going to kill her, she was, at the very least, going to make him work for it.

"That's not how it wor—" His concentration had broken, and his foot landed in a small crevasse. His ankle turned, pitching him backward. And because Erin had been pulling so hard in the opposite direction, the thrust of his backward motion was forceful.

His eyes. Erin would never forget the alarm in his eyes. In that moment, he stopped being an adversary and started being human. But, it was too late. Her snowsuit slipped through his fingers, and his arms continued to reach for something that wasn't there. She fell backward onto her rear end and instantly grabbed for the rock she'd braced herself against.

She didn't reach for him.

She didn't react to save him.

She let him fall.

His deadly roar had turned to a vulnerable scream, short and abrupt. Horrible noises ripped from him as he bounced down and down. And then there was silence.

Erin sat for a moment, catching her breath, unable to believe she was still alive. Part of her was expecting to see him come back over the edge of the cliff, hand over hand, knee up, twisted face. Undefeatable.

But he never did.

Slowly, she returned to her hands and knees and crawled toward the edge, flattening to her belly because she no longer trusted her legs to hold her. She needed to rest before she tried to move up this mountain again.

But first, she needed to see that she was safe.

She crept so she was barely peeking over the ledge, but could see nothing but darkness below. She fumbled for her headlamp, slid it on and turned on the light, swallowing away her adrenaline and fear. It shone on the snow below, at first showing her nothing, but then, as she moved the beam of light, she found him.

His body was facedown in the snow, impossibly far away, a halo of red around his head. He was still.

Erin closed her eyes to thank God for saving her.

But the moment she closed them, she heard a gunshot in the distance.

Chapter Fourteen

The sound of the shot ripped a gasp out of Erin.

"Patrick," she whispered, straining to see out in the distance, find the cabin she knew was there... somewhere.

She felt like she needed to do something. Rush to him. Be there to stanch the blood or help him run or... say goodbye. But she had no idea where he was, had nothing other than a vague location somewhere *watching the cabin*, so where would she rush to, anyway? Would she have escaped the clutches of this kidnapper only to put herself in those of his accomplice?

She'd let Jason die. She'd let the man at the bottom of the cliff die. And now, in letting Patrick—new to the mountain—go off on his own, she'd allowed him to die, too.

Who was she to call herself a rescuer? She didn't rescue. She was no hero.

If the gunshot had been aimed at Patrick, and if he was dead, she'd left Kerrington to die, as well. Surely, the man's partner in the cabin would soon figure out he was alone in his crime now. He would be desperate and afraid and probably bail on the plan. Why keep Kerrington alive for a failed ransom?

"I'm so sorry," she said, although she wasn't quite sure to whom she was apologizing. The list was too long. "I'm so, so sorry."

More than ever, she felt the pull toward her tiny chapel in the woods. She was cold and tired and regretful of everything that had happened.

She took a minute to get her bearings, turning this way and that, and then finally climbed above the tree line so she could see the trail. She knew she was on the Madison, which was good—it meant she hadn't traveled far. But she didn't think she'd be able to get all the way to the cabin from here tonight.

She did think she could make it to the chapel in the notch, though. She would rest there and figure out what to do in the morning.

Every muscle in her body ached as she descended the mountain. She shook and sweated, despite the cold and the wind. She could feel the sting of a hundred bumps and bruises, thanks to her little spin down the mountain. She feared that in the morning she would be too sore to get down to flat ground.

She made it to the bottom of the Madison and worked her way into the notch. The chapel sparkled in the clearing, almost appearing to be lit from the moon above like a spotlight was shining on it. She could see her and Patrick's tracks in the snow from earlier. It seemed like a lifetime ago.

The chapel always felt warmer than it should have with no actual source of heat. It was as if it generated its own warmth, beckoning to weary travelers. *Almost like a Christmas card*, she thought. Besides, she had her bivvy and there was no wind inside the chapel. She would be warm enough.

She ducked inside and let her eyes adjust, then pushed one of the pews up against the door. She'd seen the man lying lifeless at the bottom of the cliff with her own eyes, but that didn't mean her eyes hadn't been deceived. And besides, she'd heard the gunshot. What if the other man was out looking for his friend? Or worse, for her? Would he use the snowmobile to get to her, or would he just be an unwelcome, deadly surprise in the night?

She took a minute to warm up, then pulled off her gloves and hat and blew into her hands. It was only then that the gravity of what had just happened really sank in, pulling her until her knees buckled under its weight. She sank onto a pew and hung her head.

Everything hurt. And she was so, so weary. She couldn't get the image of the man lying in the snow at the bottom of the cliff out of her mind. She'd never seen Jason's body under the fallen arch—Rebbie had kept her from going up once they located him—but in her mind's eye, it was a similar sight. Death was somber, regardless of who died, or how. Someone, somewhere, would mourn this man's life, and she was the one who'd taken it.

Not true, she tried to argue with herself. *He fell while trying to kill you. You didn't push him.*

But she knew that she also didn't save him, and that, while it had all seemed to happen in a blur, maybe if she'd acted more quickly, he would still be alive.

And then what? He'd have killed you, anyway.

"But it's not up to me to decide who lives and who dies," she said aloud.

And that was exactly what she'd done. Twice now.

The truth was, Jason had gone up without her that day because she was mad at him. She'd been asleep; that part was true. But she'd known Jason was going up on a rescue and she had purposely gone home and lain down. Her reasoning was silly and childish.

They'd had plans for that very night—a belated celebration of his birthday. She'd bought tickets for a show in Concord, two hours away. They met at PARR and were just about to head out when the call came in. Hikers who'd been out having a great time were stranded in Tucks. Erin argued to let Kevin and Rich have the rescue, but Jason, who had taken the call, could tell the hikers were panicking. He and Erin were already at PARR, he argued, so why not go up? They could miss a few minutes of the show.

Erin had been angry. Jason had tried to console her, but it only made things worse. Next thing Erin knew, they were arguing—the only fight they'd ever had— and she was storming out of PARR, telling him to take someone else up the mountain, and for that matter, take someone else to the show. She'd gone home, taken Murphy for a walk, and gone to bed in a sulk.

She'd missed his call.

The events of the last year rushed over her full force, the feelings that had been a dull ache now a sharp stab in her heart. She'd thought she'd been completely broken, but she was still enduring blows. Whatever message she was supposed to have learned—whatever message she'd thought she had learned—was still to be revealed.

"I'm so sorry," she wailed, her face turned up to the cross at the front of the chapel. "I was selfish. I never meant for him to… Oh, please forgive me. And help me forgive myself. I know he should have called Rich. Or even Tommy. But I was the one who let him down. It was me. Out of spite and childishness. I've always thought I was having a hard time forgiving him for going into a dangerous situation alone. But…it's me I can't forgive. He trusted me and I let him down. Please, God. Help me."

After a long while, she wiped her eyes, sniffed a few times and gazed again at the cross. "Thank You for allowing me to live today. I don't know if it was really Jason whispering in my ear to fight, or if it was You, or even if it was me, and I heard my own words in Jason's voice. I just know that somehow I found the strength to fight, and that had to come from You. Forgive me for letting the man fall, and peace be with his soul."

She grew sleepy, but just as she began to drift off, the chapel door rattled, jarring her awake. She sat up straight, every cell on alert, her eyes darting around the chapel for a hiding place or a weapon.

"Erin?" She heard Patrick's voice on the other side of the door. "Are you in there? Let me in."

Chapter Fifteen

When Erin flung open the chapel door, she came toward Patrick with such intensity, he nearly flinched away. She wrapped herself around him in a viselike hug, her face buried in the shoulder of his snowsuit. He couldn't help holding her in return.

"Thank You, God," she said over and over again. She let him go, looked him over as if she was searching for something, then tipped up her head and said to the moon, "Thank You, God!"

"Shhh," he admonished, ushering her into the chapel. "I don't know how far voices can carry up here. I heard you earlier from wherever you were." He watched as she shut the door and shoved the pew against it, then turned to him.

"I thought you were dead," they both said at the same time, a moment of synchrony that bloomed deep in his chest. He'd never felt that before. It wasn't just that they'd said the same thing at the same time, but more that they felt it. It filled the entire chapel. A pulse in time.

"The gunshot," she said, pulling him toward a pew. He sat and spent a moment taking down his gaiter, removing his hat and gloves, and unzipping the top of his snowsuit just to get the snow and chill away from his chin.

He shook his head. "Wasn't even close, really. He's getting really antsy about his partner. Kept opening the doors and looking around. I could hear him inside mumbling and mumbling and then it got louder. He's starting to lose it. He finally came out and got on the snowmobile. I think he was going to go look for his buddy, but the snowmobile didn't work." He reached into his pocket and produced the spark plugs. "He started yelling that he knew I was out there, and when he found me I was going to be dead. And then he fired a shot into the trees. Way off to my left. I realized if he decided to do something crazy, like shoot Kerrington, we would hear it. So I decided to come find you. I wanted to make sure you were okay."

"How did you know you would find me here?"

He shrugged. "I just knew. I can't really explain it. And I can't explain how on earth I remembered where it was. It was weird how I walked right to it."

He realized he was still shivering, and Erin reached into her backpack and produced an energy bar. "Here. This will help you keep your energy up."

He pushed it away. "You should eat it."

"I've already had one," she said. "Please. I need you."

He unwrapped the bar and took a bite. Flavor exploded onto his taste buds and he took a moment to savor it before talking. He chewed and swallowed. "I

heard you scream. It scared me. I was afraid something horrible had happened to you."

He was able to convince himself the first scream
was just his imagination, or maybe Kerrington or even
the wind. But the second scream was definitely Erin's,
and it tore at him. He felt it as if she'd been crying
out directly into his head. He didn't want to let down
Kerrington. But he couldn't let Erin be run down by
a madman, either. He didn't really even think about
it before he'd darted out of the bushes and raced toward the sound.

He felt a dull emptiness that echoed, one he'd felt
before. He'd had a moment of grief, of wondering if
he was now without her on this mountain. But then
he'd been struck with a certainty. Not only was she
alive, but she was also in the chapel. She was there,
wondering about him. Pleading.

It wasn't a hunch; it was as if a voice had whispered
it to him. *Go to the chapel. Go, find her.*

"It was bad," she said, her eyes watery and reflecting back moonlight. "I can't even think about how
close I came to…" She closed her eyes and shook her
head. "I knew better than to play some sort of game
on the mountain. With a kidnapper, no less. As if the
mountain doesn't have potential enough to kill."

"Do you know where he is?"

She stared at him for so long and so openly, her
throat working, he knew what she was going to say
before she said it.

"He's dead." Almost a whisper.

"Did you…?"

She shook her head. "He fell," she finally said. "He almost pulled me down with him."

Patrick was overwhelmingly grateful that Erin had survived. And he would be foolish not to acknowledge that the loss of one man meant one less obstacle toward getting Kerrington out of that cabin and off this mountain.

Erin told him about the man tackling her. She showed him bruises that were just beginning to form on her arms, her face, her neck. She talked about tumbling down the mountain, and how she was sure that the worst had happened. But then a voice had told her to fight, and somehow she had the clarity to remember the pickaxe and found the strength to grab it and use it to stop herself. She told him about the man catching his ankle in a crack and the horrible sounds he made while falling to his death.

Then they sat in silence for a very long time. The chapel grew darker around them as they sank deeper into the night, their limbs heavy and their minds sleepy. They pushed the pews against the walls and got out their bivvys, spreading them on the floor and climbing inside for warmth, their heads sticking out.

Patrick turned to his side so he could face Erin. "Can I say something I've been thinking about?"

"Sure." Her voice was soft, as if she was just on the edge of falling asleep.

"I think I was meant to be here," he said. "I think I prayed for it."

She turned onto her side, too, facing him. "You… prayed for this?"

"Not to run across a kidnapped teenager and spend

a day running for my life, no," he said. "But I prayed for the chance to even the score."

He was aware of her presence next to him: warm, inviting, understanding. She'd laid herself bare with her story. It didn't seem fair for him to keep his own story to himself, regardless of how painful it was. If they both died on this mountain, at least one other person might have understood him. And, he discovered, that mattered.

"Even the score with who?"

"With the mountain," he said. "It—it took my sister. Well, not this mountain specifically, but one just like it."

"Oh, Patrick, I'm so sorry. I had no idea."

"It was a long time ago."

"Is that why you wanted to become a rescuer? To even the score with a mountain?"

He nodded. "But really, I think I was meant to even the score with myself."

"I don't understand."

He'd never shared this story with anyone outside his family and their attorneys. His mother had forbidden anyone to speak of it. When they buried Hannah, they'd buried everything with her. Including history. But he never stopped carrying it with him. And, he supposed, he never stopped wishing for someone else to know.

"It was my twenty-first birthday," he said. "We had a huge party at a ski lodge in Lincoln. My parents basically rented out the entire lodge for our family, plus about twenty friends. It was a great time and we were hanging out all night, long after our parents went up to bed. And somehow, the conversation got on to who was better on the slopes—my sister or me. We were both really good, and both really proud of it. And we were bantering around so I challenged her, right then and there in front of everyone. I knew how to get keys to the lift, so we went up around three o'clock in the morning, and when we got to the top, we argued again about which slope to ski. She wanted to go down the easier one, since it was nighttime and we couldn't see great. But my ego was on the line, and I suggested we ski off-slope, since we were looking to see who could handle the snow best. I kind of forced the issue. So…we did."

Erin put a hand to her mouth, eyes wide. "Oh, no."

"Long story short, she never saw the tree she hit, because it was so dark. She just went full force into it. Exactly like she was afraid of."

"Oh, Patrick, you had no way of knowing."

He swallowed. He could see Hannah's face right in front of him if he closed his eyes. It would be seared into him forever. Her nose was bleeding profusely, and her cheekbone had been split. But it was mostly the gurgling sound of her breathing that haunted him.

"She had no idea what happened or why she couldn't move or even feel her body. She didn't really seem to know where she was or how she got there. It was obvious how bad it was, that she was in shock and probably had a brain injury or…" He shrugged. "But she knew me. She recognized me." He glanced at the cross at the front of the chapel. It seemed to beckon him to continue, to bare his soul. "She begged me not to leave her. But what could I do? I couldn't help her, and I couldn't get her down the mountain in the shape she was in. We didn't have any way to communicate with anyone else. Only our friends knew we were up there, and they were too busy partying to notice we'd been gone a while. I had to go back down without her and get help."

"So they brought in a mountain rescue. Someone like us."

He nodded. "Yeah, but by the time they got there, she was gone. Massive internal injuries. My family has never forgiven me for that. Not only that I goaded her into the challenge in the first place, and that I was the one who decided we would go off-slope, but mostly that I left her there to die alone. I never told them about her begging me to stay. It was bad enough for me to live with that. My mother didn't need to know it."

Erin reached over and squeezed his hand, then left hers there, holding his tenderly, as if to convey through their palms alone that she understood and was here for him. "So it's more than just 'evening a score,'" she said. "You wanted to get into mountain rescue to make up for what you couldn't do then."

"I think so, yes."

"But you didn't know she was going to die. You can't blame yourself for what you didn't know."

"Everyone else blamed me. That's why I work for the family business. I'd already disappointed my parents so much, it seemed like taking the job they wanted me to take was the least I could do. But when you're twenty-one, you really don't realize how long a lifetime can be, you know? Especially a lifetime of doing something you hate."

"You shouldn't do that to yourself. You should for-give yourself and do what you want to do. Follow your dreams, not what you think you should be doing out of some sort of punishment for an accident."

He offered her a grateful grin. How had he ever considered her as cold or closed off? She was open and kind and forgiving. He should have seen that first. And might have if he hadn't been too busy looking out for himself. Suddenly, a woman he'd only met a day ago was the one person he didn't want to stop being around. "Can I ask you a question?"

"Sure."

"Why are you leaving?"

She closed her eyes. "Like I said, it's too hard to look at this mountain every day and know I lost some-one I loved here. Because of my own doing."

"But what about what you just said to me about my sister? You had no way of knowing, either."

She hesitated, reopening her eyes and looking deeply into his, conveying so many messages with-out saying a word.

He leaned closer. "Did you know?"

"No, of course not. It's just… I knew he was going up alone."

She told him a story about arguing with Jason right before he went up the mountain. By the end of her story, she seemed spent, as if she'd just been wait-ing for the opportunity to get that off her chest—for someone to confess to. The thing was, it didn't change Patrick's opinion at all. In fact, it only made him ad-mire her more.

"I understand your feelings," he said. "But—" He'd

been about to say "but I don't want you to leave," but had been unable to wrap his mouth around the words.

"But what?"

"But…I can see why you need to leave." Inside, he felt crushed. It was the total opposite of what he wanted, but he couldn't tell her that. She was resolute and he respected that, regardless of how it made him feel. Besides, who was he to say that she even felt the same way about him that he felt about her?

Yet…either he was imagining things, or she was also crushed on the inside. He could feel some pull between them. He knew it was there, because he'd never felt anything like it before. It was as exhilarating as flying down a mountain on a pair of skis. And equally dangerous. If he didn't know better, he would think Erin wanted him to tell her not to go.

It's just wishful thinking, Patrick, he told himself. *She's crushed because she lost her friend and you're reading into it.*

The moment stretched and snapped, and they were back to reality again. In a cold, abandoned building surrounded by deadly wind and a deadlier kidnapper.

"So what do we do from here?" Erin asked, and the haze of the moment shimmered at Patrick from a distance, with the slim possibility that she was referring to their feelings for each other. But he realized she meant what would they do about Kerrington.

"I can't leave her up here," he said.

She gazed at him. "Neither can I."

"They've hit her. She was in bad shape when I checked in on her. I don't know how long before the man who's got her just gets rid of her. We have to come up with a plan. We've got to get her out of here."

They both flipped to their backs and stared at the chapel ceiling.

"I think he's going to go looking for his friend in the morning," Erin said. "That will take him out of the cabin. We can use that time to free her."

"But what if he doesn't? He knows there's someone out here," Patrick said. "How can we be sure?"

"Right. We can't. Unless we could flush him out somehow."

"Or lure him out."

"There are two of us and one of him. Think we could we force him out?"

"He has the gun, remember? Even if we brought our axes, we would have to get too close."

She thought it over, nibbling on her bottom lip. "We could make him think his friend needs help."

"The other snowmobile," Patrick said. "We can use it. Do you remember where it is?"

She thought for a minute and then nodded. "I remember where the cliff was. It can't be too far."

"I'll start the snowmobile and yell for help. From a distance, he probably won't realize it's not the right voice. In the meantime, you make your way to the cabin."

"As soon as he walks out, I go in," Erin said.

"When he gets to the snowmobile, I'll lead him away, back down the mountain," Patrick said.

Erin shook her head. "No. No way. No more splitting up for us. We stick together. We go down that mountain together, no matter what."

Patrick paused, then said, "Okay. As soon as he heads for the snowmobile, I'll come back to the cabin."

"I'll take the spark plugs and put them back in so we have a working snowmobile."

"Yes," he said. "I'll get back up to the cabin as soon as I can to help you."

"And then we get on the snowmobile and go down together," Erin said.

Patrick nodded, but couldn't pinpoint exactly why he had such an uneasy feeling about this.

It would be a real surprise if it all worked out as planned.

So far, almost nothing had.

Chapter Sixteen

All night, Erin had nightmares. In most of them, she was being chased. Didn't take a Freudian scholar to figure out that one.

In the last one, however, she was doing the chasing. But she wasn't chasing a person. More like chasing a clock. Chasing time.

She was running for Tuckerman Ravine, a pair of concert tickets in her hand, which were slowing her down.

Dream Erin got to the ravine and instantly spied the snow arch. It wasn't collapsed, and Jason and the hikers weren't trapped. They were standing in the arch, gazing at how awe-inspiring it was, and Erin couldn't help pausing to appreciate its beauty, too. Everything was okay. Everyone was okay.

Perhaps the last year had been the dream. A very bad dream. And this, this moment in the ravine, was real life.

But then she felt a tremor. Instantly, she knew what it was. She tried to call out—*Jason! Get out of there!*—but he couldn't hear her. She tried to run, but her feet were encased in ice. She tugged at her boots, panting and grunting with the effort to free them. Little by little, the ice cracked around them, but with every crack of the ice around her feet, there was an echoing sound of the arch cracking. Just as she finally pulled loose, the arch fell, burying all that were inside.

"No!" she yelled, running, stumbling, sliding backward, stumbling again.

When she finally reached the arch and fell to her knees, frantically digging at the snow with her fingers, she unearthed a face.

Only it wasn't Jason.

It was Kerrington. Her nose was bleeding, her cheek split.

"Don't leave me," she begged, very much alive.

But Erin turned from her and dug more, unearthing another body.

"Jason," she said, and worked even more frantically, her arms burning. But when she got him uncovered, she realized he was facedown in the snow, a halo of blood around his head, and they were no longer under the arch but at the bottom of a cliff, with Erin looking over a ledge high above. It couldn't be. She would have known if that man was Jason.

She turned him over and it wasn't Jason at all. Or the kidnapper.

"Patrick?"

He was clearly dead, and she ran her fingers through his hair, filled with deep mourning. But then his eyes popped open and bore right into hers, and he said, "Go without me."

Erin woke with a start, sucking in a great gasp, and spent a dizzying moment trying to make sense of where she was, why she was lying in her bivvy on a cold, wooden floor wearing her snowsuit and gloves. She blinked and turned over, taking in the cross at the front of her favorite little chapel, the light pouring in through the windows beyond it, and everything came back into focus. She sat up with a start.

Patrick stirred next to her, then sat and reached for her. "What's wrong?"

She realized she was still breathing as if she'd been running across the icy ravine, and there were tears on her cheeks. She stared at him gratefully. He wasn't dead. He hadn't fallen off the cliff. He was right here next to her.

"Nothing," she said, swiping at the tears, trying to simultaneously swipe away the residual feeling of terror. "Bad dream."

"About what?"

"Nothing. It's fine. Just a dream. Did you get any sleep?"

"Not really," he said. "I didn't want us to be surprised in the night. You?"

She shook her head. "What I wouldn't give for a cup of coffee right about now. Even the mud that Rebbie makes. Oh." Saying Rebbie's name out loud reminded Erin that her office manager must have been going crazy waiting to hear from her.

She opened the backpack she'd been using as a pillow and pulled out her radio. "Rebbie? It's Erin."

There was a pause, and then… "Erin! You're there!

Thank goodness! You had us so worried, you wouldn't even believe."

Something about Rebbie's voice gave Erin a sense of calm and relief, as if it was some sort of proof that they would be down the mountain by afternoon, standing in the overly warm PARR office. This would all be over, and they would be safe and together again. Erin wouldn't even mind doing the paperwork if it meant she was on flat land.

Rebbie's voice crackled through again. "Are you safe?"

"We are. We're holed up in the chapel."

"We?"

"Patrick is fine, too."

"Thank goodness. And the girl?"

"She's still in the cabin with the kidnapper."

"So now what?"

"We have a plan. We're going to get Kerrington down today." It felt weird saying it aloud, as if maybe someone else was talking. Someone else would do the saving. Erin and Patrick would stay here in the chapel, warm and safe, and would come down once everything was over.

But she knew nothing would happen unless they made it happen.

"And her kidnappers?" Rebbie asked. "What about them?"

"There's only one left." Erin squeezed her eyes shut, willing away the image of Dream Patrick lying in the snow. "We're working on a plan for the other one. What's the wind like?"

A pause, and then the voice of the sheriff broke through. "Erin, I'm sorry. It's still too strong."

"I understand," Erin said, and she did, she just bitterly wished she didn't have to.

Rebbie's voice came through again. "I had to order Tommy to stay on the ground. He was fixing to come up there when we didn't hear from you last night. I told him the last thing you wanted was for him to crash trying to get to you."

Erin smiled. Good old Tommy. It seemed like forever ago that her biggest problem was figuring out a way to get him to agree to take over PARR. Hard to believe it was only two days ago that she was meeting with a real estate agent and breaking it to Roberta that she'd be moving away.

"I'll be sure to thank him for the thought when I get back," Erin said. "*Today.*"

"What do you need from us?" Sheriff Grimes again.

"I just need you to stand by at the bottom of the Madison. Maybe have an ambulance there, just in case. Look for us in a couple of hours, I would guess. Over and out."

There was a crackle—Rebbie trying to get through again—but Erin switched off the radio and stuffed it back into her pack before she lost her nerve and told them she wanted to come down now.

Patrick had readjusted his gear and was standing in the middle of the chapel, his head down, hands clasped in front of him. His lips moved as he said a silent prayer.

He'd told her the night before it was a sermon that

convinced him he needed to join PARR. That he'd been withholding himself. That even though what they'd stumbled into was horrible, he was thankful to God for leading him here.

He said he was thankful to God for leading her there, too.

They'd locked eyes for a long moment after that. Erin understood how much they had in common, and how wrong she'd been about him when they'd started. Her heart had fluttered in that moment.

And it was fluttering again, as she watched him extend his gratitude. She bowed her head and offered a quick thank-you, too. They had more things in common than she'd originally thought. Important things.

When Patrick's prayer was over, he slid his gloves onto his hands and turned to her.

"Are you ready for this?"

She shook her head. "I don't think anyone could ever be ready for this."

He nodded in agreement. "But if anyone could, it would be the great Erin Hadaway, mountaineer extraordinaire."

She offered a weak smile, but even that belied how she was really feeling. For some reason, all she felt was doom.

It was the dream. It was just the dream making you feel that way.

That, and she was starting to feel weak from the strenuousness of the climbing they'd done with no real food or drink to sustain them. She knew a body needed fuel, especially in this type of weather, where it was burning extra calories just by shivering. She wondered how much longer either of them could continue without real replenishment.

They gave their gear a final once-over and wordlessly set out into the cold and wind again, heads down, feet trudging forward through the snow.

Erin had never felt unsteady on the mountain before, and often didn't understand how people were too frightened to come down a traverse they'd just gone up. But now she understood it. When you didn't feel stable, the mountains seemed much higher.

The only way to get down was a one-inch step of faith at a time.

Slowly, slowly, they made their way, stopping every so often to gaze down at the cabin, once it was back in view. They watched for movement, listened for sounds and signs that something—anything—had changed. But there was nothing. It was almost as if they were the only two up here again.

When they got to the bottom of the mountain, they slipped into the trees, wandering, looking for the abandoned, working snowmobile.

"It has to be around here somewhere," Erin said, going over her own footsteps for the third, fourth, fifth time. The wind had pushed snow around overnight, filling in the dead man's footsteps, making it even more difficult to find this needle in a haystack.

"Maybe the other one already came and got it," Patrick said, but they both knew they would have heard the noise of the motor running. They were counting on that noise to make this plan work.

"No, it's here. I know it is." She turned and studied the cliff face. It had all seemed to take place so long ago. "Where exactly did we go up? Do you re-member?"

He pointed. "That ledge up there. You can't really see it from here, remember? We had to step forward to watch him."

Erin turned so she was aligned with the ledge, then, as much as she didn't want to, closed her eyes and visualized the man coming toward her. She had to squeeze them tight to keep them shut—they wanted to automatically spring open in terror. His face, even in her mind's eye, reminded her of falling down the mountain, afraid she would be unable to stop herself. The wrench of her shoulders as she tried to hang on to the pickaxe. She felt a moment of intense longing to be at the bottom of the mountain, the whole night-mare behind them.

Them.

In this longing, she imagined them as a *them*. She'd known she'd been feeling it, and she was pretty sure he had been, too, but they were too in-the-moment to examine it head-on. And besides, what did it mat-ter? She was leaving Gorham and he was just getting settled there.

Her eyes flew open. She pointed. "That way. He came from those trees right there."

It was an area they, of course, hadn't yet gone over. But after just a few minutes of walking, they found it, parked in between two trees, hidden from plain view just as it had been when they'd first discovered where the snowmobiles had been parked. The tracks had led Erin and Patrick to Kerrington. And to each other.

"We need to get it out of these trees," she said.

"Can we move it without turning it on?" Not waiting for an answer, she grabbed the handlebars and dug in deep, giving it all she had. It didn't budge. "Not just the two of us."

"I'll drive it out," Patrick said. "I'll take it to just inside the edge of the woods."

They both turned and looked at the tree line. They couldn't see the cabin from here, but they knew it was right on the other side. Not far at all. Once Patrick started the engine, if everything went as planned, they would only have minutes until the remaining kidnapper showed up.

"It all seemed so much easier last night when we were laying it out," Erin said. "Now that it's real, I'm scared."

Patrick reached down and clasped her hand with his. "We've got this. We have to. For Kerrington."

"For Kerrington," Erin echoed. "You're right. We've come this far." She turned and faced Patrick. "You've been amazing. You're a natural. You're going to be a huge asset to PARR. I think I made assumptions about you, but I was wrong." And then, echoing what he'd said to her on the day they met, she said, "Color me impressed."

He beamed. "You sure do have a rigorous first day of training. Maybe go a little easier on the next new guy? Glad to know I passed, though."

She tapped her temple as if she was thinking this over. "Hmm…nobody said anything about passing. I mean, you didn't even make it up Washington."

"Neither did you."

"I could climb it with my eyes closed."

"I could ski down it with my eyes closed."

"I could solo climb the whole traverse before you could even get up the Jackson. Child's play."

"Well, I…" He thought it over. "I could develop a ski resort town right here around this cabin."

"Uncle. Uncle."

They both cracked up. Nervous laughter. They knew what they had to do, knew what the stakes were. If they messed up, Kerrington could die. Or they all could. Erin took a breath.

"Are you ready?"

He nodded and pulled up his gaiter.

"Okay, give me about ten minutes to get into place, then go for it," she said. "I'll hurry."

"Don't be fast, be safe."

"I will." She pulled down her goggles, pulled up her gaiter and gave him a thumbs-up.

But just as she turned to leave, she felt him tug lightly on her sleeve, stopping her. She pushed up her goggles again.

"Don't leave," he said.

She gestured toward the cabin. "But I thought the plan was—"

He shook his head. "That's what I meant to say in the chapel. What I wanted to say when I said I understood why you needed to leave. I meant to say 'but you can't leave the mountain when I just got here.'" He swallowed. "I don't want you to go."

The wind gusted, and it was as if it had ushered in all the emotions Erin had been holding back in regard to Patrick. She'd been keeping herself from feeling them, but they were undeniably there.

She didn't want to go. There were deeper feelings between them, feelings that would be wonderful and exciting and right to explore, and all she had to do was stay in Gorham.

But she'd already made her decision. The plans were already in place. And she'd made them because the pain of staying was just too great.

Sometimes too late was simply too late.

"I have to. I'm sorry," she said.

Patrick's face fell. But more than that, it was as if his entire soul fell. She could feel it more than see it. He pulled away from her, distant and hurt. A lump formed in her throat, a desire to reach out to him. To let him know she felt the same way he did. To let him know that she was protecting him.

But he simply nodded, turning back to the snowmobile. He wasn't even angry, and that was the part that hurt the worst. Anger would have meant he didn't understand her.

"Ten minutes," she said, unsure if her words were even loud enough to be heard over the wind.

He nodded again and straddled the snowmobile.

She turned and walked away.

Chapter Seventeen

Erin knew good and well that she could make it to the cabin in far less than ten minutes.

She had padded her time so she could reach out to PARR one last time before executing their plan, and she wanted to have that conversation alone.

She found a niche between rocks that held the wind back and lowered herself inside it. She pulled down her hood and gaiter and produced her walkie-talkie from her backpack.

"Rebbie? It's Erin. You there?"

Rebbie answered immediately. "I'm here. What's going on? We're going crazy here. Are you okay?"

"I'm fine. Patrick's fine. We're setting up. I just…" She stared out into the trees, their leaves dusted with snow, swaying in the wind, and thought, as she had a thousand times before, how beautiful the mountain was.

"How come you're always up there, Hooves?" her granddad had always asked her, and she would just shrug. She could never quite put into words exactly what it was that drew her to the mountain. But as she grew into adulthood, she began to understand.

The last time she was home, her granddad was still alive. And when evening fell and she began lacing up her hiking boots to head out into the mountains, he asked her once again, "What is it about them mountains, Hooves?"

"They're so big, Granddad," she'd answered. "They make me feel small. There's something comforting about that. Knowing there's always something out there that's bigger than me, and that it was created by someone who is also bigger than me. It's like sitting on God's lap up there."

And despite what happened with Jason and Kerrington, she still felt that way. She didn't know where she would find that comfort when she left.

"You still there?"

Erin was jarred back to the present. She pressed the button on the side of the radio. "I'm here. I just wanted to say goodbye."

"What? What's going on? Talk to me, Erin. Are you in trouble?"

"Just in case things don't work out, you know? Everything's fine right now, and we have a plan, but I want to make sure everything is covered just in case. I want Tommy to take over PARR, okay? But I want you to run it with him. Nobody knows the ins and outs like you do. Tell Rich it's nothing personal—it's just that Tommy's been with us longer, and he's got rescuing in his heart."

"Erin—"

"And do me a favor. After I leave, take care of Patrick. He's amazing at this and…well, he's just amazing. Just like you said he'd be, Rebbie. He's going to be a great rescuer. He needs this."

"Erin, stop talking like you're—"

But she was committed now, and she had to finish what she was saying. She knew this wasn't a just-in-case scenario. It was going to happen. She was saying goodbye, regardless of what happened up here. "He's still going to need training, but he'll get it quick. Which is good. We need to always have a couple ready to mobilize at any time. From here on out, nobody goes up alone. Promise me that, okay, Rebbie?"

"Erin, you're going to come back." Erin could hear tears in Rebbie's voice. More than that, she could hear fear.

"Just promise me."

"Okay, sure, nobody goes up alone. When you get down here, we're going to laugh about this conversation, you know," Rebbie said. "And you're going to owe me the biggest piece of pie from Franny's for worrying me like this."

Erin smiled. That sounded like a great idea. Maybe she would invite Roberta. And Tommy and Rich and Patrick. A whole pie party. A goodbye pie party.

"Deal," she said. "I've got to go. We're starting our plan now."

There was another pause, and then Rebbie said, "Erin, please be careful."

Erin turned off the radio and stuffed it back into her backpack. Rebbie was right—it wasn't fair of her to worry them like this. But saying goodbye was easier from a distance, and it had to be done one way or another.

She got up, dusted the snow off her suit and headed toward the cabin, hiking at a fast clip to make up for lost time.

The cabin appeared through the trees bit by bit. Mottled and hidden and lovely, like if she knocked on the door, a pack of singing elves might spill out of it and invite her inside for a hot dinner.

She was acutely aware of the bright orange of her snowsuit in that moment, realizing she would stand out against the green and white all around her. If the man looked out the right window at the right time, she would be a huge target. How far could his gun shoot, and how good of a shot was he? She didn't want to find out.

She dropped her pack, unhooked her harness and stepped out of it, then steeled herself for the cold before shucking off the snowsuit. Any experienced winter climber was layered, but losing the extra layer made it feel as if she was wearing shorts and a T-shirt. She wrapped her arms around herself and watched the cabin for any movement inside, trying to assess what might be the best way to approach. She felt, rather than saw, someone watching her. She ducked and kicked the snowsuit farther into the trees.

She must have waited longer than she thought, or Patrick started too early, or her conversation with Rebbie had gone on longer than she'd realized, because suddenly she heard the kick and buzz of a motor farther down the mountain. The hairs on the back of her neck stood up.

"Here we go," she whispered, shifting from foot to foot, preparing to run.

"Help!" Patrick yelled, and even though she knew it was a ruse, that this was part of their plan, she still felt a jolt, a yearning to go after him and make sure he was okay. "Help!" he yelled again.

But shockingly, there was still no action coming from the cabin. "Come on, come on. Aren't you even curious?" Maybe they weren't fooling him. Maybe he suspected it was a trick.

Suddenly there was shadow movement inside the cabin and a man's face appeared in the window, peering out directly at her.

She gasped and sank lower, wishing she hadn't chosen such an obvious hiding place. Had he seen her? She couldn't tell. And she wasn't sure if she had the energy reserves to play a deadly game of tag on the mountain again. Actually, she was sure that she didn't.

But the man scanned the area left and right. Then he disappeared from the window, and moments later, the front door opened.

"Bingo!" Erin whispered, relieved. If he'd seen her, he would have let her know for sure by now.

Instead, he stood in the doorway and continued searching the forest with his eyes. He was young. Very young. Couldn't have been much more than a teenager. And he looked an awful lot like the other man. *Father and son?* Erin thought. *My goodness, what a horrible family legacy.*

"Help me!" Patrick cried. "I'm hurt!"

"Dad?" the man called, proving Erin right. "Dad? Is that you?"

Of course, even if it had been his dad on the snowmobile, he wouldn't hear his son calling for him over his own noise. If he wanted to know, he had to go to him.

The young man cursed, disappeared into the cabin and came back out, pushing his arms into the sleeves of a coat.

Erin's heart soared. He was falling for it. He was doing exactly what they wanted him to do. *Go, go, go*, she thought, and then, when he disappeared from her sight, thought the same thing to herself: *Go, go, go!*

She no longer felt the cold, even though the wind threatened to knock her sideways. All she thought about was getting into the cabin. She raced, running as hard as she could, praying that no rock or snow-buried stump would reach up and break her ankle. She bolted across the clearing and into the cabin, slamming the door behind her.

Kerrington gasped and cowered, surprised by the slam.

"It's okay, it's okay," Erin said as she looked for something to push in front of the door. She finally settled on a kitchen chair that looked like it might fall to kindling if she tried to sit on it. Hopefully it would withstand the pressure of a door trying to open, if need be.

She ran a circle through the cabin, making sure all of the windows were locked, and ended up in the tiny room where Kerrington remained bound.

The teen looked as if she had lived a thousand lifetimes in one day. And, Erin supposed, she probably had. Her wrists and ankles were bloodied from where they were bound, and her socks were missing, her toes a cold bluish gray. Her face displayed new abrasions, too. Erin felt sick at the thought of the girl getting a beating because Erin and Patrick had been here.

"Please," Kerrington whined. "Please help me."

Even her cries had less fervor behind them than they had before. *She's running out of gas*, Erin thought. *Or else she's giving up.* Either way, it was time to end this.

Erin grabbed another rickety chair and dragged it to the back door, propping it under the doorknob. Kerrington's sobs rose the farther away Erin walked, turning into panicky gasps. Erin wondered how long it had been since the girl had had anything to eat or drink. How much longer would she last on this mountain? Erin wished she'd at least brought some water from her pack. She let the thought drive her harder. The faster she freed Kerrington, the faster they would get out of here, and the faster she would get all the care she needed.

Distantly, Erin heard the motor cut off. She paused, listening, but all she heard were Kerrington's cries.

"Shush, shush," Erin said, and when she didn't hear anything outside, she sprang into action. "We've got to go. Fast."

She dropped to her knees behind Kerrington, the hard floor sending bright stabs of pain up Erin's shins. The tumble down the mountain had bruised her more than she'd realized. She gritted her teeth against the pain and bent over the rope that was tying Kerrington's hands to the stove. The girl's struggles and cries grew louder and more frantic.

"Get me out! Untie me now!"

Erin shushed and shushed, dropping into the calm mode she knew so well. You couldn't panic on a rescue, or you were likely to make a mistake. One that could be deadly for you and the person you were rescuing. On top of that, if you were rattled, the person you were rescuing would be more likely to panic, and panic plus mountain always equaled disaster. You had to lead your rescue to the same calm place you were in.

Plus, it just made it easier to concentrate.

She scooted so that she could look into Kerrington's face. The haunted, streaming eyes that looked back at her nearly broke her heart. It would be years—if not a whole lifetime—before this girl would be okay again.

If, that was, they even got her down alive.

"Kerrington," Erin said in her most soothing voice. "You have to calm down. We need to be able to hear what's going on outside, and I need to concentrate on these knots, okay? Be as still as you can be."

The girl nodded, sniffling, but she was shaking too hard to be anything even resembling still. Erin had to work with what she was given and be grateful that at least the screaming had stopped.

She went back to the knot, tugging on the mess of rope and examining it, trying to decide where to even begin.

"I'll tell you what the plan is, okay?" she said, in part just to keep Kerrington quiet and connected. She kept her voice low so Kerrington would have to remain quiet in order to hear her.

"Okay," Kerrington said in a scared, shaky voice.

"When I get you out of these ropes, we're going to

get on the snowmobile outside and get you down this mountain. Are you strong enough to hold on if the ride gets rough?"

Kerrington nodded.

"Are you strong enough to climb if we get to a spot the snowmobile can't traverse?"

She nodded again, although they both flicked dubious glances at her bare feet. Who knew what damage the cold had already done, but walking through the snow would only make certain that she would lose toes to frostbite. A physical forever reminder of what had happened to her.

But Erin had to remain optimistic, for Kerrington's sake. They would take climbs and frostbitten toes as they came. They would deal with them when they had to. Besides, they hadn't really looked around the cabin. There were lots of discarded things here. Maybe they'd find a pair of abandoned shoes, or a blanket they could tear and fashion into a coat. Perhaps some plastic to tie around her feet. There were possibilities for Erin to work with. She just had to get Kerrington free in order to explore them.

"Good. You'll be home by this evening…"

Erin trailed off as she located the knot and began fumbling with it. She was no stranger to knots. She'd been through more ropes rescue trainings than she could count and had grown up with brothers in Scouts. She'd taught classes on knot-tying. So she knew right away that the kidnappers were also no strangers to knot-tying. She hissed through her teeth as she tugged and pulled on the rope.

"What's going on?" Kerrington asked.

But before Erin could answer, there was a thump, and Kerrington screamed, the sound long and shrill, as she stared up at the window. Erin turned to look.

And saw a figure staring right back at her.

Chapter Eighteen

The figure shifted and the change in lighting showed his face. It was Patrick, gesturing for her to let him in. Erin was filled with relief.

"It's okay, it's okay," Erin said as she abandoned the rope and rushed to the back door.

Patrick came in on a gust of wind that nearly took away Erin's breath. She hadn't realized that in her concentration, she'd actually begun to sweat.

"The motor stopped," she said.

"I stopped it," he said. "I realized we were making escape way too easy on this guy, so I drove it farther into the trees, parked it and walked away."

"What?" Erin asked. "But what if he just comes back here?"

"He probably will," Patrick said. "But first, hopefully, he will look for his dad. And maybe he'll try to start the engine without the key. Either way, we have a little bit of time on him, and once he gets back here, we'll be gone. We need to move."

"Okay, help me," Erin said, going back to Kerrington. "You untie her ankles while I get her hands. They tied this with a gunner's knot."

"What's...?"

"It's a constrictor knot. They knew what they were doing. The harder you pull on it, the tighter it gets and the less likely you'll ever be able to pull it apart. Some people say you can't untie a constrictor knot."

Kerrington whimpered.

"Can you?" Patrick asked.

"I don't know," Erin said truthfully. "I've never really tried until now. It helps that I know how to tie one. That way I know what needs to back out first." She grunted as she worked the rope with her fingers, Kerrington's blood coloring them, making them slippery.

Patrick knelt by Kerrington's feet, and in just a few moments, those ropes were released. She tried to stand, yanking on the knot Erin had been loosening. She flopped back onto the floor with a *floomp* of moaning.

"Don't get up!" Erin said. "Stay put, Kerrington. Wiggle your toes to get the feeling back in them."

But Erin knew that not moving was easier said than done. The girl was full-on sobbing now, her legs curled up underneath her. Freedom was so close, yet they all knew if the man came back now, she would still be captive. Just like last time.

Erin's fingers shook. They didn't want to cooperate.

"Come on, come on," she said.

"I'll get our ride ready. The spark plugs?" He held out a hand. Erin glanced at it, then felt her entire body go slack.

"What?" she asked, as if she hadn't heard him correctly, even though she knew she had.

"I need the spark plugs so I can get our snowmobile up and running," he said.

Erin's fingers were throbbing from trying to pull apart that knot. None of this was going as planned.

"They're in my backpack," she said.

"Okay?" He swiveled to look around the cabin.

"It's in the woods," she said, crestfallen. This was the worst mistake she could have made. "The walkie-talkie is in there, too. Everything is in there."

They stared at each other for a long moment, and Erin knew he was thinking exactly what she was: they were doomed.

"I'll go get it," Patrick said, turning to leave.

"No," Erin said, jumping up and going after him. Kerrington cried out indignantly, but Erin ignored her. "It's too dangerous for you to go back out there."

"It's too dangerous for me to *not* go back out there," Patrick said. "That snowmobile is our way out of here. I have to go."

Erin knew he was right. Even if she could manage to untie Kerrington, they would still be stuck here without a way to get down. She felt sick knowing that there was a working snowmobile just down the mountain in the tree line, and that they had not only given it to the man who wanted them dead, but had also lured him to it. And they were the ones who disabled this one.

They should have come in the night. Or before dawn. They should have already fixed this one.

She kicked herself for being so unprepared in a

rescue. Her only solace was that she'd left her snow-suit with her backpack, which would make it easy to spot in the woods.

"Okay," she said. "But take off your snowsuit."

He glanced down at himself.

"You're an easy target in that orange," she said. "That's why I took mine off. You need to try to blend in. Let me show you where mine is. Find it, and you'll find the backpack."

She led him to a window on the opposite side of the cabin, leaving an enraged Kerrington still tied to the stove, and pointed.

"Just inside those trees. I had to kind of kick it back, but it's not far."

"Got it." Patrick slipped out of his snowsuit and headed for the door. "I'll be right back."

"Be safe," she said, before shutting the door behind him and barricading it. She leaned against the door and gave a quick, silent prayer.

Please, God, keep him safe. And help me untie this knot. Help us get out of here.

Chapter Nineteen

The place where Erin had pointed was taking him farther into the woods than he wanted to be. She'd been smart to remove the snowsuit. The orange was easy to spot. But leaving the spark plugs was a mistake he only hoped they could recover from. He paced the area, eyes firmly planted to the ground, urgency welling up in him with every second he couldn't find it.

Finally, he spotted a bit of orange behind a pair of spruce trees, the backpack a few feet away, nestled in the snow. He grabbed it and headed back toward the cabin as fast as he could, trying to step in his own past footsteps to keep his pace. The more tired he got, the less sure his footing.

Patrick knew he had done a good job of weaving the snowmobile into a mess of trees that would take time for the kidnapper to get out of, especially since he had taken the key with him. But he also knew that a snowmobile could be hot-wired just as easily as a car, and he knew that the kidnapper was determined, so his time was limited.

He was just about to break through the tree line when he heard a rustle of footsteps and the unmistakable click of a gun cocking.

"Where is he?" the boy asked. He couldn't have been more than seventeen. He was only a few feet away, and the gun was leveled directly at Patrick's chest. "Where's my dad?"

Patrick stopped and held up his hands. "Don't do anything you can't take back, son."

Patrick knew better than to stop and engage, but part of him felt sorry for the boy. Had he ever really had a chance in life, or was this always going to be his destiny? How much blame could he take for what had happened with Kerrington?

"Where is he?" the boy repeated, louder this time.

"You can stop this now. Just let her go."

The boy waved the gun, stabbing the air with it in Patrick's direction. "I'm not going to ask you again."

"He's gone," Patrick said.

The boy gritted his teeth. A grimace or a smile? Patrick wasn't sure, but it was chilling to see nonetheless. "You killed him."

Patrick shook his head. "No. He fell."

"You're a liar!" the boy yelled. "You killed him."

The boy was losing control. Had perhaps already lost it long ago. Patrick needed to end this. "It's over. You can't finish this alone."

"I can finish this," the boy said, tightening his grip on the gun. "I can finish you."

Patrick reached into his pocket and pulled out the snowmobile key. He held it up, dangling it between his thumb and forefinger. "You can just leave," he said. "Just get away."

"So the cops'll be waiting for me at the bottom? I don't think so."

"There are so many ways down this mountain. How would they possibly know which one?"

"Helicopters."

"They can't fly in this wind. They would have already been up here if they could." He could feel the boy relenting. He took a step closer. "They'll never find you." Another step. "I have no idea who you are, so I can't lead them to you." Another step. He tossed the key to the boy. It bounced off his chest, startling him. Patrick watched in what seemed like slow motion as the key disappeared into the snow, then the boy steadied his gun and fired.

The kick of the gun knocked the boy back a couple of steps, the surprise on his face mirroring the shock on Patrick's. Neither of them could believe he'd taken the shot, it seemed. But, shocked or not, Patrick wasn't going to give up this opportunity to get out of there.

He bolted before he even realized he'd been hit. He felt a hot sting rip across his biceps, and then his arm went numb. But his legs were fine, and he was more convinced than ever that if they wanted to survive, they needed to get off this mountain now.

He moved in a crouch, half expecting to hear the crack of a gun and feel the whiz of a bullet flying past him. Or worse, to hear nothing and feel nothing until after a bullet had reached him and he fell, dying, in the snow. He tucked his head down and ran for the cabin.

There was no second gunshot, and he could only

hope that meant the boy had heeded his advice, taken the key to the snowmobile and made a run for it.

He needed to get these spark plugs back into this snowmobile so they could make their own escape. But the numbness had worn off, and now his biceps burned and ached, and his arm felt wet inside his sleeve. He noticed a small patch of blood droplets had formed in the snow under him. But it was a patch, not a pool, and Patrick tried to take comfort in that.

He had just taken the hood off the snowmobile when, in the not-far-off distance, a motor started.

So the boy had gone for the other snowmobile. He only hoped this meant he'd taken his father's death as a warning, and that self-preservation would kick in and the kid would turn downhill and light out for his escape now.

But he had a feeling that wasn't going to happen.

Chapter Twenty

If Erin hadn't been in such a daze after seeing the man at the bottom of the cliff, she wouldn't have accidentally left her pickaxe behind, and maybe Kerrington would be freed by now. But she'd left it, which meant she had to untie what was universally considered an impossible knot. The longer she fiddled with it, the less cooperative her fingers became, and the more hopeless she felt. Sweat ringed her forehead and temples now, while at the same time, her cold fingers felt stiff and unmoving.

And Kerrington wasn't helping at all. She continued to pull against the rope, cutting deeply into her skin, tightening the knot. Her wrists had started seeping a decent amount of blood, making the rope even slicker on top of everything else.

Erin supposed she couldn't blame the girl. It had to be incredibly nerve-racking to be this close to being freed, yet still be bound. And who knew what horrors this girl had already endured?

What was worse, she couldn't tell if the noises she

heard coming from outside the cabin were Patrick working on the snowmobile or the other kidnapper coming back. Her mind began playing tricks on her. She was certain that Patrick was dead in the woods, and that the kidnapper stood between her and those spark plugs. She and Kerrington would meet their end together.

She had to distract herself from those thoughts so she could focus on the impossible knot.

"Kerrington, do you go to church?" she asked.

"Wh-what?"

"Church. Do you go?"

"I don't know. Sometimes, I guess."

"Good. Do you know any hymns?"

"What? I don't understand."

"Songs. Do you sing songs at your church?" The rope loosened the tiniest bit. Erin's heart thudded into action. She tried not to get too excited and pull in a way that would bind Kerrington tighter.

"Yeah."

"Sing one to me," Erin said.

"What? I can't—"

"Please. It'll calm me down." In reality, Erin knew it would calm down Kerrington, too. Giving her something to concentrate on other than trying to get out of the cabin would be a good thing. Erin had used this technique more than once while rescuing. She'd joined in on more rounds of "Row, Row, Row Your Boat" while waiting for Tommy to arrive than she could count.

"Um. I don't know. Um." And then Kerrington

started to sing, her voice childlike and touching. "'When peace like a river, attendeth my way…'"

Erin joined in, her fingers feeling warmer and stronger with every word. "'When sorrows like sea billows roll…'"

Kerrington started to cry but kept singing through the tears. "'Whatever my lot, thou hast taught me to say 'It is well, it is well with my soul…'"

"Good," Erin said as the rope slid another millimeter. "Good choice. One of my favorites. Keep going."

But Kerrington broke off during the chorus, listening. "Is that him?" she asked.

"Keep singing. I almost have you."

But Erin couldn't help wondering if she really did. It had felt like this knot would never budge, and now that it was, it still felt like it wouldn't budge enough to become loose. *Don't give up*, she repeated in her head. *Don't stop.*

She tugged and yanked, twice breaking fingernails to the quick, her own blood mixing with Kerrington's. She ignored the pain and kept going. She didn't notice that Kerrington had finished the song. But Kerrington noticed something else far more sinister.

"Is the sound…? Is he getting closer?" she asked urgently.

Erin cocked her head and listened. Yes, the noise of the snowmobile was definitely getting closer rather than farther away. The clock was ticking faster and faster.

Her forearms strained as she pulled, and miraculously, the rope came free.

For a moment, she simply stared in disbelief that she'd successfully untied a gunner's knot.

"What?" Kerrington asked.

"I got it," Erin said.

Kerrington jumped, trying again to get to her feet, and again falling back to the floor, yanked down by the rope around her wrists.

"Hold on, I've got to unwind it." She was already fiercely unwinding the rope as she said this. Kerrington moved her arms and wrists to help the process, then cried out with relief when the rope fell to the floor. She brought her hands to her chest, rubbing her wrists repeatedly. Erin swept Patrick's snowsuit off the floor and held it out. "Put this on. And get your socks. We need to go." She searched the cabin for something to use as shoes while Kerrington wriggled into the suit and socks, but only managed to find a filthy and ripped pair of old socks. "Better than nothing," she said, tossing them to Kerrington, who layered them over her wool socks gratefully.

Patrick was struggling to put in the spark plugs when they came outside. He motioned for them to stay low.

"What's going on?" Erin asked.

"My arm doesn't really want to cooperate, and my hands are numb from the cold," he said.

Only then did Erin glance at his arm and notice the patch of deep red that had soaked through the sleeve of his jacket. She gasped.

"You're bleeding!"

He nodded.

"He shot you? Are you okay? Is it bad?" She reached for him but came short of grasping his arm.

"I don't think so. I haven't looked, but I'm still standing, and that's all that matters."

"What can I do? Do you want me to put that in?"

He shook his head and gestured to the blood-smeared backpack. "I'll get this. You should get on the radio."

"Good idea." Erin grabbed the pack and pulled out the walkie-talkie with one hand and a bottle of water with the other. She offered the water to Kerrington, who accepted it and drank from it greedily as the motor in the distance grew louder and took on a strange thumping noise.

Patrick snapped the spark plugs into place and quickly worked to get the hood back on.

"It sounds like he's coming toward us," Erin said.

"I guess he doesn't want to leave any witnesses." He screwed in one screw but dropped the second one into the snow. He brushed his hand around in the snow to find it.

"Do you think he still has the gun?"

He produced the second screw, covered in flecks of snow, and worked it into its place, his hands shaking so hard the screw chattered against the plastic before sinking into its hole. "I know he does. And he's obviously not afraid to use it. But he's not good with it. His aim isn't great, and he can't handle the kick. If we keep moving, I think we'll be fine."

"Either way, we can't stay here. We've got to go," Erin said, and not for the first time, began to really question whether they would make it down alive at all.

There was no time to radio for help. She quickly slid the walkie-talkie onto her belt.

Patrick gave the screw a final twist and stood, just as the other snowmobile popped out of the woods and headed straight for them. "Quick! Get on," Patrick said.

Erin wasted no time straddling the seat. It had been a minute since she'd driven a snowmobile, but in some ways it was like riding a bike. She gave a quick mental rundown: throttle, pull cord, kill switch...

"Key," she said aloud, placing her finger over the empty ignition. She whipped around. "Patrick. There's no key."

She knew there was a way to start older snowmobiles with no key. But that required pulling out wires, and she wasn't even sure which ones. The kidnapper was getting ever closer. There was no time for that.

"The other one had two keys on its key chain. I kept one," he said. "They should be interchangeable."

He stood and reached into his pocket. The kidnapper was more than a dot on the horizon now. He was closing distance quickly and bearing down on them. There was definitely a pulsing sound coming from the motor's noise—Erin couldn't quite figure out what it might be, but she hoped something was wrong with the engine. Maybe it was getting ready to die.

But the pulsing wasn't weakening. It was only getting louder.

"Get behind me and duck down," she told Kerrington. The girl obeyed, her breath coming out in nervous, rapid little puffs. She wrapped her arms around Erin and buried her face in Erin's back. Erin could feel her shaking.

It seemed like Patrick was taking forever. But it was probably only milliseconds before he pulled the key out of his pocket and tossed it to Erin.

She knew he was right—there were only so many snowmobile keys made. They were often interchangeable. But there was a part of Erin that doubted this key would work. It seemed everything about this rescue plan had gone wrong, from start to finish. This would be one more wrong thing.

Her hands were shaking so hard, the key jittered and clacked around the keyhole for what seemed like hours. She used her other hand to still the shaking one and slid the key into place. It fit.

She glanced up; the kidnapper was only yards away from them now. Close enough that she thought she could see a scowl on his face that matched his dad's scowl. It threatened to freeze Erin, but she fought against it, working frantically.

She turned the key and pulled the cord.

Nothing.

"Come on," she said, glancing up again. Now she couldn't quit looking at the approaching vehicle. *This must be what deer feel like when a car is bearing down on them*, she thought.

She pulled the cord again.

Nothing.

"No," she said. "This can't be—" She pulled again. Nothing.

She glanced; the kidnapper was close enough to use the gun if he wanted to. But he would have to stop in order to take any sort of aim. If he stopped, she would bail and go back inside the cabin. Regroup.

The radio squawked on her belt. "Erin? This is Rebbie."

The thumping and thudding grew louder and started to take on a familiar quality.

"Erin?" Rebbie's voice was barely audible over the noise of the motor, the *whump, whump, whump* on the horizon, the wind, Kerrington's whines and the shiver of fear that ran through Erin.

Whump, whump, whump...

"The choke," Patrick said. "You forgot to release the choke."

He was right. In her hurry, she had forgotten to pull the choke to get gasoline to the engine. Without hesitation, she pulled it out, then forced herself to do a mental checklist again.

Kill switch off. Choke out. Key turned.

She pulled the cord.

The snowmobile putted to life. She nearly cheered out loud, but there was no time for celebration.

"Let's get out of here," she said, but then she noticed that Patrick had walked several feet away from the snowmobile. He was facing the approaching kidnapper. "Patrick! Get on! We can make room!"

But he waved her away.

"Erin?" Rebbie's voice only floated on top of the surrounding noise. "Tommy...risk... Landing point... flare?"

Too many things. There were too many things for Erin to concentrate on just one. She felt like she was being pulled apart as she tried to make sense of everything.

"Patrick!" she called.

He turned, and she knew what he was going to say before he said it. "Go without me," he said. Just like the dream. And, just like in the dream, her gut felt leaden, her heart torn out of her chest.

She shook her head. "We go down this mountain together, remember?"

"We're not far enough ahead. Get out of here. Get Kerrington out. I'll pull him away."

"But how will you...?" She trailed off, because she knew the answer. He wouldn't get down the mountain alive. He knew it, and she knew it. And, likely, the kidnapper knew it, too.

Whump, whump, whump!

The thumping sound, which Erin now realized was a sound she knew deep in her bones, grew louder. She looked up just in time to see Tommy's helicopter, struggling against the wind, pop up over the ridge.

"Go!" Patrick yelled. He didn't wait for another argument. Erin watched as he ran toward the kidnapper, waving his arms. Sacrificing himself. Leaving little droplets of blood on the snow behind him.

She was distantly aware of something pounding on her back. Kerrington, urging her to get moving. But she couldn't tear her eyes away. Patrick got dangerously close to the snowmobile, then veered away, around to the other side of the cabin.

The cabin sat in a little bowl. On every side, there was a rise of some kind. Tommy was heading toward the rise to the east; Patrick was running up the rise to the west.

"Go!" Kerrington yelled into Erin's ear.

She glanced up. She could see Tommy leaning forward over his controls, his face lined with determination as the helicopter shuddered in the wind. It was the thought of the wind snatching Tommy out of the air that finally got Erin moving.

She grabbed her radio. "Up top! Up top! There's a level spot up there. We'll meet you!"

She squeezed the throttle and took off over the bumpy snow, Kerrington's hands momentarily slipping from around her waist and then finding grip again.

There was something about the pounding rhythm of Tommy's helicopter that filled Erin with calm. By the time Tommy arrived on the scene, Erin was pretty sure the rescue would be a success. They'd never lost someone when they worked together. Tommy was daring and Erin was sure-footed, and all whomever they were rescuing had to do was follow orders.

But right now, she hated the overwhelming chopping of the blades against the wind because it, combined with the growl of her motor and the wind in her ears, drowned out everything else. She had no idea where the other snowmobile was, or what Patrick was doing to keep the kidnapper occupied. She feared he would let the snowmobile run him down, or even let the boy shoot him again.

He would die up here so she could live.

She knew before she'd even crested the ridge that she couldn't leave Patrick up here, injured and in danger.

She wasn't going to leave this mountain without him.

Chapter Twenty-One

❧

Patrick only had time to think three things:

1. He must be crazy.
2. He wished he'd had the chance to tell his mother that he loved her at the end of their last conversation.
3. Erin would survive without him. Someone would make her a wife, and it wouldn't be him. He'd never know the sweetness of her kiss.

It was this last thought that filled his chest with heaviness. He wanted her to survive, no matter what. That was the objective. If someone was going to get to the bottom of this mountain alone, this time it wouldn't be him.

But he'd wanted to make it down together. Get another chance to tell her his feelings for her.

And here he'd thought he'd come up the mountain to even the score. Turned out the mountain wanted to score another point against him. Game over.

Still, he was sure this was his fate. What God wanted for him. And he knew without a doubt that he would rather have died on this mountain than live forever at a desk selling real estate.

And besides, who was to say he wouldn't make it, anyway? He was far from giving up. He pushed himself harder, knowing the kidnapper would be on him in moments.

He ran in a serpentine pattern just in case.

Right as Erin and Kerrington took off, the PARR helicopter rose over the ridge, more gigantic in the air than on the ground. He could feel the beating of the rotors in his chest, as if his heart had synced with it.

The helicopter swayed as the wind gusted, but the pilot was determined to keep it in the air. Swayed and corrected, swayed and corrected.

Erin had taken the snowmobile up, her arc perfectly matching the helicopter's path. The two worked together like dancing a complex ballet they'd perfected over years, and had he not been running for his life, he might have wanted to stop and watch. He might have found himself even more in love with her than he already was.

Every time he glanced over, she was farther along, leaning forward over the handlebars, pushing the snowmobile faster and faster.

She would be over the ridge and out of his sight in moments.

And then what?

What exactly was his plan here? His lungs were reminding him that he couldn't run forever. He would have to stop and face the boy flying behind him. And what would he do? This seemed pointless. Running to nowhere. And it would be no time before the terrain was no longer something he could run on. He wasn't good enough to scale back up the cliff quickly. Not without Erin.

He could almost hear his mother in the back of his mind, admonishing that this was exactly the reckless type of decision-making he was famous for. He didn't think things through before acting on them. He got people killed.

Except this time, he was saving someone. Two someones.

And getting himself killed.

Sadly, he doubted even that would be enough to satisfy his mother. She'd made up her mind about him on the day of Hannah's accident, and it would never change. No matter how much he tried to conform himself to fit her idea of the "right kind" of son.

He took one last glance at Erin just as she and the helicopter both dipped below the ridgeline on the other side. He could just barely see the chopper blades whirling over the top of the ridge.

She'd made it.

He made decisions quickly, that was true. He didn't always think things all the way through for every possible thing that could go wrong. He thought on his feet.

And that wasn't always a bad thing.

If he could get back to the cabin, where his gear was lying crumpled on the floor, maybe he could use his pickaxe as a weapon. At the very least, he would force the boy off the snowmobile and even the play-

ing field. He could stop running before his body gave
out on him.

He abruptly U-turned and started back the way
he'd come, passing the snowmobile in a wide arc as
he did so. The boy, clearly much more versed in riding than shooting, stood and swung his leg over the
seat so that both feet were on the running board, going
into the turn without missing a beat. He turned hard,
attempting a roll-up, but he'd turned too sharply. The
snowmobile chewed into the snow and stopped, giving Patrick an extra moment. He ran, clenching his
teeth and waiting for the gunshot that would certainly
come, the pain of another bullet entering his body.

Patrick felt no pain and heard no gunshot. Instead,
he heard the throttle of the snowmobile motor, and
glanced back to see the boy barrel-rolling the sled out
of its stuck position. He glanced in the other direction
and saw the helicopter rise over the ridge again, fighting the wind as it pointed its nose downhill. He could
feel the rumble of the blades churning the air, the noise
drowning out his own breathing. But as the helicopter
sped away, he realized the noise didn't shift with it.

It wasn't the helicopter he was hearing. Or the
snowmobile. It was something else entirely.

It seemed to come at him slowly, at first a strange
knocking sound, and then a roar.

And a rumble.

He made eye contact with the boy on the snowmobile—he was frightened, angry, trapped and sorry—
and then he was down, his entire world blotted by
white.

Chapter Twenty-Two

Erin pushed Kerrington into the helicopter far less ceremoniously than she would have liked to. But the gunshot had rattled her. There were two men on the other side of that ridge. One of them had a gun. And it wasn't the one she might be falling in love with.

She didn't have time to feel grief or fear, or notice the cold that was whipping into her with each blade rotation. All she felt was a deep need to get back to Patrick.

Kerrington climbed inside and scurried far away from the door, making room for Erin. But Erin shook her head.

"You go!" she shouted to Tommy.

"Get in here!" he shouted back. "You're going to freeze to death out there!"

She shook her head again and made waving motions with her arms. She didn't have time to argue with Tommy. She had to get to the other side of the ridge.

The wind kicked up and the helicopter swayed.

"You're not even supposed to be up here. Get the girl down. Leave me!"

"There's room for both of you!"

"Patrick is down there!"

She could see the realization dawn on Tommy. He knew—everyone knew—how guilty Erin felt about what happened with Jason. He knew she couldn't let Patrick be down there alone, not after that.

"I can't, Tommy! I can't leave him."

Even if he's... She couldn't finish the sentence, even to herself.

Reluctantly, Tommy gave her a thumbs-up. She shut the door, then crouched down and ran back to her snowmobile. She took one moment to watch Tommy lift off and swing the helicopter toward the base of the mountain.

She's saved, Patrick, she thought. *We did it.*

But the victory felt bittersweet without Patrick here to experience it with her.

As the helicopter flew away, she pulled out her walkie-talkie.

"Rebbie, it's Erin."

"You don't sound like you're in a helicopter, Erin." Of course, Rebbie already knew Erin wasn't in a helicopter. Tommy had certainly relayed that information immediately upon lifting off with Kerrington.

"I know. Listen, I don't have time to explain. I just wanted to make sure law enforcement is waiting at the bottom of this mountain in case the kidnapper tries to go down."

"Which direction?"

"We're on the south side of the mountain, but I don't

know exactly where he is. I only know that he's armed and has used his weapon. And…" She hesitated, resting the radio against her shoulder so she could catch her breath, could make her mouth form the words. "And we'll need an ambulance. Patrick has been shot."

Even though she knew he wasn't gravely injured, saying the words out loud gutted her.

"You need to come down."

Erin didn't answer.

"Erin? Promise me you're coming down."

She didn't want to make a promise she wasn't sure she could keep. All she knew was that she and Patrick were stronger together. They'd vowed to get down this mountain together, and if Erin had anything to say about it, that was exactly what they would do.

She clipped the radio back to her belt and gunned the snowmobile toward the ridge.

Just as she neared the top, she was heartened to see Patrick still running, high up on an adjacent ridge, heading back toward the cabin. The kidnapper had bailed from his sled in what looked like a failed turn-out. He was busy trying to roll the sled out of its predicament, but before he could get any real momentum, his hands were ripped from the handlebars of his machine and he disappeared—sank, really—into a cloud.

She felt her snowmobile shake against the ground, as if she was treading over a bed of rocks. But she knew the snow was deep here; she'd gone over it smoothly just a few moments before.

She slowed, confused, but the quaking worsened. And when she stopped altogether, the vibration turned to rumbling. He hadn't been veiled by a cloud; he'd been sucked under by snow.

"Patrick! Avalanche!" Erin yelled, even though she knew she was too far away and the noise from the rolling snow made it far too loud for him to hear. But he seemed to realize what was happening, and glanced backward quickly before racing down and to the left. He was heading for the trees, trying to get out of the path of the deadly slide. But he was too slow. Nobody outran an avalanche.

Erin watched in horror as the snow lifted him from his feet and tumbled him under, so quickly it was almost as if she'd imagined it. He disappeared, just as the kidnapper and the snowmobile he'd been riding on had.

Afraid of kicking off a chain reaction and ending up in her own deadly slide of snow, Erin angled the snowmobile away from Patrick and took it down the hill into the notch. Avalanches could be fast—sometimes traveling as quickly as eighty miles per hour—and by the time she reached the bottom of the notch, the rumbling had stopped. She looped toward the cabin and took her ride as close to the newly piled snow as possible.

When she turned off her vehicle, the silence was unbearable. No motors, no helicopter, no cries for help. So many times, over so many rescues, Erin was aware of how elegantly that beauty and danger comingled in places like this one. How quickly tragedy settled into a postcard photo. Fluffy white snow cascading through trees with a rustic cabin backdrop. So lovely. So deceptive.

But Erin didn't have time to marvel right now. She slipped off the snowmobile and raced toward where she last saw Patrick. Already, it had been at least a minute. If he was crushed under pounds and pounds of snow, the seconds were ticking. He needed air.

"Patrick!" she called, dropping to her knees and pawing through the snow, hoping he would be able to make a noise so she could find him. "Patrick!"

She dug a foot or so and found nothing, then moved to another spot and dug there. And then another and another. She saw a handlebar poke through the snow, and nearby, a piece of fabric.

"Patrick!" she shouted and ran to the fabric.

She pulled and ripped at the snow with everything she had, a flurry of swinging arms and hopeful heart. She was breathing as if she'd just sprinted a mile. She didn't even feel the cold. She felt no wind at all. She felt only terror and urgency.

When she finally uncovered the fabric, she discovered that it was a stocking cap. Not Patrick's cap.

Instinctively, she lurched back, as if the kidnapper was going to spring out of the snow and come after her. But, of course, he didn't. He wasn't moving at all. In fact, she could now tell that the buried snowmobile was on top of him. He'd been rolled under both snow and machine.

Her hands hesitated over the snow. She'd found a person, and she was obligated to try and save him. It wasn't just because of her oath as a rescuer; it was her personal oath as a fellow human. It wasn't up to her to decide if someone was worthy of saving. This man had caused so much pain and destruction. And

Patrick, who'd been nothing short of heroic, was still waiting to be found. Every second that she spent unearthing this boy was a second that Patrick was potentially without oxygen. She didn't want to waste time saving this evil man.

But she knew that Patrick would have done it. He wouldn't have wanted to any more than she did. But he would have done it, regardless. Because it was the right thing to do. A life was a life, after all, and they both had suffered over loss. They both knew the horror of losing someone you love in an accident. Surely, someone loved this boy. Maybe someone innocent; maybe not. That wasn't for Erin to judge.

With shaking fingers, she dug the snow from the face attached to the hat, uncovering one closed eye, and then the other, a snow-packed nose, a slightly open mouth.

"You're so young," she said aloud. Probably just following orders, trying to be a "good son" in a very wrong way. "Are you with me? Hello? Can you move? Do you hear me?"

But she already knew. His neck didn't look right. It was more than crooked. Bent in a way that suggested there was no way he could possibly have survived it. He was gone. So young, and gone—and for what? A failed kidnapping, where the best he might have hoped for was a little money that would probably be spent long before he reached full adulthood?

"Why were you so desperate?" she whispered, tears collecting in her eyes.

It wasn't grief for the boy, though. Not entirely. It was also the grief that accompanied her dawning certainty that if she found Patrick, she would be looking into another still, bluing face. She'd never even had the chance to fully admit that she was falling in love with him. How could she say goodbye when she'd barely had a chance to say hello?

But then, over her soft sniffling, she heard a noise. A…voice? No, she was imagining it.

She continued digging, her arms and legs and entire body aching and tired from the work of the last two days. She heard the noise again.

She sat up on her heels. "Patrick?" she asked, softly, almost as if she was afraid to say his name out loud and make the hope real. But when she heard what she thought was her name, faint but very real, she jumped to her feet. "Patrick? Patrick! Where are you?"

He called for her again. Yes, now she was sure he was calling for her. And she followed his voice, asking him to yell again and again, until she reached a mound in the snow near the very edge of the drift. He'd almost made it to safety before the snow pulled him under.

"Say something again!" she said, her heart in her throat as she turned every which way trying to find a clue to where he might be.

"I'm here."

She scanned the mound and found a hole on the back side, Patrick's head and one shoulder and arm sticking out, darkening the snow with blood. His breathing was labored, crushed out of him by hundreds of pounds of snow. It must have been taking a monumental effort to be heard.

"I've got you," she said. Back down to her knees she went, as she set about shoveling snow with her hands once again. Gone was the fatigue that had just set upon her. She felt light and filled with hopeful adrenaline.

"Watch. Watch for him—" Patrick said.

She shushed him. "Save your oxygen. He's gone."

"He could come back."

She leaned forward and shoved an armful of snow away from where Patrick's middle was trapped.

"No," she said softly. "He's...*gone*. I found him over there. I think the fall may have broken his neck. I'm not sure if maybe his snowmobile rolled over him on the way down."

"Kerrington?"

"Is probably at PARR right now, drinking some of Rebbie's famous hot chocolate with her parents." Not likely. Kerrington was much more likely to have been whisked away by ambulance, getting pumped full of fluid and looked over for injuries, her parents waiting for her arrival in a cold, sterile waiting room with paper cups of junk coffee. But Erin liked the image of Rebbie giving her some TLC much better.

"She got down," Patrick said, a confirmation more than a question. "Rebbie was right. You are a super-hero."

"Thanks to *you*," Erin insisted, pausing to look into his eyes. "I'm thinking maybe you're the super-hero here."

"Thanks to us," he said. She couldn't really argue with that. It had been teamwork, through and through.

"Thanks to us," she agreed. "Now shush until I get you out."

It only took a few more minutes of digging before he was able to wiggle his way free. Finally, he was lying on top of the snow, taking in long, deep breaths while she radioed base.

"Rebbie? I've got Patrick," she said, a breathy laugh bubbling up and escaping before she even realized it was there.

There was a pause, a crackle, and then Rebbie asked, "I'm sorry, can you repeat that?"

Erin's laugh intensified and turned to tears. Giddy, elated tears. "I said, I've got Patrick. He's alive."

"That's what I thought you said! They're both alive!" There was a cheer in the background. "Injuries?"

Erin glanced at Patrick, who had gone to moving his limbs and rolling his wrists and ankles. "Nothing broken, I think," he said.

"No broken bones, but one gunshot graze," Erin said. "Some bleeding, but not critical."

"Tommy says he thinks he can get back up there. You want to meet him in the same spot?"

Erin paused and looked at Patrick, who was now sitting. He made eye contact with her and held it. So many emotions flooded Erin. So much comfort and familiarity. It was as if she'd known Patrick her whole life. And maybe in some ways she had.

"Erin? You copy?"

Patrick didn't need to say a word. Erin already knew.

"I'm here. Tell Tommy to hang tight there. We don't need the ride."

"You sure?" Rebbie asked.

Erin and Patrick grinned at each other.

"Yeah," she said. "We got up here together, and we're getting back down together. We made a promise."

Patrick stood, walked over to Erin and held out his good hand. She took it and let him pull her to standing. Getting back down was going to take energy she wasn't sure either of them had. But she was too elated to care.

"Okay," Rebbie said. "Then get down here already so I can hug you!"

Erin and Patrick chuckled. Everyone should have a friend who cared as much as Rebbie did. Erin brought the walkie-talkie to her lips.

"I'll see you at the bottom, Rebbie. Over and out."

Chapter Twenty-Three

There was a celebration at the bottom of the mountain. Rebbie brought a huge thermos of hot chocolate, and Patrick sat inside an ambulance, downing cup after cup until he felt sick. He was the kind of cold that ached deep into his bones, and his muscles felt shredded after all that climbing and then the fall.

He had to admit, the avalanche was terrifying. All of it was terrifying, and he would probably see Kerrington's frightened cower every time he closed his eyes for the rest of his life. The poor girl—how would she ever move on from what she'd experienced?

People were resilient. He knew that much. They somehow kept going, even when it seemed like they had no reserves left. They pushed against the pain and put one foot in front of the other, and wasn't he proof enough of that himself?

He was right about the bullet—it had only grazed him. The paramedics had cleaned and bandaged the wound, and he had promised to have it looked at first thing in the morning. Kerrington had been whisked away before he and Erin arrived at the bottom of the mountain, but somehow, he and Erin both came away from the ordeal with just a few bumps, bruises and scrapes—all of which hurt less than saying goodbye to each other.

Nothing broken, except my heart, he thought.

They'd been ushered to separate ambulances to be checked over, just in case.

Rebbie climbed into Patrick's ambulance and sat on the little seat across from him.

"Well, you sure know how to show off on your first rescue," she said. "Does it hurt?"

He glanced at the bandage on his arm and shrugged. "Not really. It will heal."

"And you'll have a cool scar," she said with a wink. "Seriously, though. I'm glad you're okay. You guys had me scared to death down here. I almost came up after you. And this girl does not climb." She waggled her fingers in the air. "My manicure is way too expensive for that."

He'd mimicked the finger-waggling. "Mine, too." He held up his cup with the other hand. "Thank you for this, by the way. It's a lifesaver."

"Oh, that reminds me, I came with food, too." She fumbled in her purse, pulled out something in a silver wrapper and handed it to him with a sheepish shrug. "It's a Pop-Tart. It's all I had in my desk."

He took the pastry. "It's perfect. You really are the force that keeps this thing running, aren't you?"

She tilted her head to the side. "What can I say, I love my rescuers. You all are part of my extended family."

They were distracted by the doors of the other ambulance slamming. Tommy slapped the side of the vehicle and waved it away. It left, empty, with lights off, sirens silent. Erin, who'd sent them away, shrugged out of the blanket that had been wrapped around her and followed a reporter to a lighted spot nearby, a man with a camera at the ready.

"She's not going to be happy about that," Rebbie said. "She usually avoids the press like the plague."

"They're everywhere," Patrick said, gesturing at the still-crowded parking lot. "That's why I'm in here, not out there."

"Hmm." Rebbie sipped her hot chocolate. "I thought you were hiding from Erin in here."

"Why would I be hiding from her?"

Rebbie raised one eyebrow. "Seriously?"

"Seriously," he said, but he knew he'd been caught. "We've been side by side for an entire day."

She nodded. "And now you're not, and neither one of you knows what to do with that."

"She's leaving PARR, Rebbie."

Her lips turned downward. "I've been wondering if she would. There've been hints. And you're staying?"

"I have no choice," he said. "I've only just gotten started on this development project."

"Which development project? The houses...or the girl?"

"Very funny—" he began, but they were interrupted by Tommy, who'd ducked his head into the ambulance.

"You've got a reporter out here who'd like a word," he said. "You up to it?"

Patrick sighed, and downed the last of his hot chocolate. No, he wasn't up to it. But even talking to the press seemed like a whole lot less of a spotlight than his conversation with Rebbie.

An hour later, he and Erin parted ways, quietly and awkwardly, the impossibility of being together pulling against both of their deep desires to do just that. She was leaving the mountain and he was staying, and that was that. There didn't need to be any more talking. The things that had happened up on that traverse didn't change anything, except for the pain of losing each other. If only they'd met sooner.

It had been over a week, and they hadn't spoken since. What could he say that would make a difference?

Besides, he had to drive home to New Castle for his mother's party. As much as he didn't want to.

He spent the whole drive thinking, and with every mile that took him farther away from Erin, he began to think more clearly.

He'd scarcely allowed himself to grieve the loss of Hannah, because he felt so responsible. But being responsible for an accident didn't make it hurt any less. He'd always felt the need to shoulder the burden because his parents had been so blindsided by their loss. But he'd neglected to recognize that he'd also been blindsided. So had Hannah. Nobody expected it to happen. That was what made it an accident.

And that was also what made the trajectory of his life afterward so unfair.

He'd made the decision about what he must do before they'd even reached the end of the trail. Maybe he'd made the decision while he was trapped under all that snow and ice after the avalanche.

He'd escaped the constricting cold of an avalanche; now it was time for him to shrug out of the constricting cold that had been with him ever since that night he lost Hannah on the ski slope.

He had to park at least a block away from his parents' house, because when Linda Rogers put on a gathering, it wasn't so much an invitation as it was a demand. Everyone who was anyone showed up, eager and excited to be inside the Rogers home, regardless of the event.

Even when the "party" was a bit morbid.

He imagined the invitations—parchment so white it hurt the eyes, smoky gray calligraphy that scrawled out the words: *Join us as we celebrate the life of our dear Hannah on this anniversary of her passing.* Perhaps a very faint and subtle set of pink angel wings just barely shadowing the background, or maybe something floral.

His sister was not an angel-wings or floral kind of person, but that didn't seem to matter. The invitations always looked the same.

When he entered the foyer, he was greeted by muted laughter, clinking dishes and soft jazz. He could smell butter and charred meat in the air, maybe seafood as well, and sugar. They were bringing out the best of the best, as they always did. Hence, the eager crowd.

The living room was packed full of beautiful people, almost none of whom Patrick recognized, holding tiny plates and making small talk. He didn't see either of his parents, but he did see, across the room near the fireplace, a tripod holding a giant photo of Hannah, forever frozen at age nineteen.

He walked to the photo and contemplated it, as always fighting a pang of guilt that lived just beneath the surface. Like Erin digging him out of the avalanche, this photo dug out those feelings. Hard. So very hard.

"Great party, Haha," he said, using her nickname. "For real. Mom outdid herself. You deserve the best." He absolutely meant it. She did deserve the best. But what he'd learned from his experience on the mountain was that it wasn't her death that made her deserve the best—it was her life. And even though she died that night and he didn't, he wasn't any less deserving of the best than she was.

When he looked back, he supposed that was what his pastor had been trying to tell him that day when he stayed behind to chat about the sermon. Not just that he should cast his bread upon the waters, not just that he should stop regarding the clouds, but that he deserved to do those things. He *deserved* life.

As if thinking about him had summoned him, Pastor Elmer wandered in from the kitchen, holding a mug.

"There's hot apple cider in there," he said, gesturing over his shoulder with his thumb. "You should get some before it's gone. It's absolutely delightful. Your mother has thought of everything."

"She always does," Patrick responded, holding out his hand for a shake. "It's good to see you, Pastor."

"Good to see you as well. I heard about your week.

You're all anyone can talk about around here. Is it true about the Hadley girl? You saved her?"

Patrick ducked his head. He hadn't wanted the story of his involvement to spread. He wasn't up on the mountain for glory and had hesitated even giving his name to the reporters who'd swarmed PARR afterward. But names had a way of getting out, especially when you didn't want them to. He had already been more than aware that the rumor mill was churning away at home. He'd been fielding phone calls from well-intentioned friends all week.

He offered a smile. "I think we saved each other."

The pastor nodded knowingly. "Did you even know you needed saving?"

"I think I did. Remember the sermon you gave? I stayed after and talked to you about it."

"I do. You cast your bread upon the waters, it would seem."

"More like I looked away from the clouds and got drenched by the storm."

Pastor Elmer laughed. He shook his finger. "I like that. I think I'll keep it in my back pocket for later."

"Feel free. And thank you."

"I've done nothing. Have you thanked God?"

"Every single day."

"That's all that's necessary." He regarded the photo of Hannah. "Your sister was a bright light of a person."

Patrick liked that, the idea of a person as a light. "Yes, she was."

"Sometimes I think that when a person shines so brightly, their light never really goes out."

Patrick nodded. "I'm sure she's lighting up the dance floor in Heaven as we speak."

"Probably," Pastor Elmer said. "But I'd really rather think she's still shining here on earth. She's just shining through you."

"Through me? Oh, I doubt that."

The pastor put his hand on Patrick's shoulder and gave it a squeeze. "That girl you saved on the mountain wouldn't doubt it for a second. Try to see yourself through her eyes. Not through the lens of guilt. You've lived with it long enough, son. The tree has fallen, and in the place where it fell…"

"There it lies," Patrick said, finishing the thought, taken aback. He was so accustomed to carrying the burden of Hannah's death, he never even considered he was carrying her memory, too. When he remembered Hannah, all he could ever see was her dying face. Why was that? Why didn't he remember her the way she was in this photo? Daring, courageous, loving, smart…and crazy about her big brother. Her accident was horrific and terrible, but it was over. He could either carry her grief or her light. It was clear which was the better option.

Pastor Elmer took a sip of the cider and smacked his lips. "This is really delicious. You should get some."

"I'll do that," Patrick said. "But first I need to find my parents. Have you seen them?"

"Your mother was in the dining room last I saw. And your father was entertaining in the piano room."

"Excellent. Thank you. It was great to see you, Pastor."

The pastor nodded and turned toward the photo of

Hannah, regarding her intently while he sipped away at his cider.

Patrick couldn't find his father in the piano room, but his mother was in the dining room, talking with some distant cousins whom Patrick hadn't seen since last year's anniversary party. Her eyes flicked to Patrick, then back to her guests. He waited until they noticed him, and then there were smiles and backslaps and handshakes all around.

"I'm sorry to interrupt," Patrick said after they'd all done the obligatory greetings. "I'm wondering if I might have a word with my mother."

"Of course," said his cousin Ellie. "Just make sure we get a chance to chat later, okay?"

The cousins filed out, leaving him with his mother, who didn't look pleased or even grateful to see the son who'd almost been buried alive just a week prior.

"Well, that was rude," she said.

"My apologies, but I need to talk to you."

"I'm here. What is it?"

"I need Dad, too. Do you know where he is?"

She narrowed her eyes at him. "Have you gotten yourself into trouble?"

"No," he said, trying to keep the edge out of his voice. He reminded himself that this was a hard day for his mother, for obvious reasons, and she didn't mean to come across as unkind as she did. "It's just… you and Dad both need to hear this, okay?"

His father walked by the dining room entrance at just that moment. "Pat," his mother said. "Pat. Come here. Patrick has something to say."

"Son." Pat Rogers stuck out his hand, and somehow the handshake was more formal than the one between Patrick and Pastor Elmer had been. "I'm glad you made it. I've heard it wasn't easy."

"Uh, no," Patrick said. "It definitely was not."

"Perhaps you'll give up on this mountain business once and for all," his mother said dryly. "You don't have the best history on them."

"That's actually what I wanted to talk to you about." Nearby, someone told a joke, and a whole group of people burst into laughter. "Can we go in the study, maybe?"

His parents exchanged wary looks, but they made their way to the study nonetheless, with Patrick trailing behind them, quietly acknowledging guests and ducking their curious stares along the way. When he shut the study door, it was as if the party wasn't happening at all. This was his father's alone space, and one reason he loved it was that it blocked out all the noise of the world. He rarely let anyone else in, including Patrick.

His mother perched on the front edge of a chair, while his father leaned against his desk, his arms crossed over his chest.

"What's going on?" he asked.

"I wanted to tell you before I told the board," Patrick said. He'd expected to be nervous or feel guilty, or any number of strange feelings, but he was surprisingly calm and resolute. This was what he wanted. It was what he needed.

"Business?" his mother said. "You pulled me away for business? You know that is conversation for your father, Patrick. I've got guests."

She started to get out of her chair, but Pat put his hand out, his eyes never leaving Patrick's face. He seemed to be able to sense his son's seriousness. "Go on, then, Patrick."

"I'm leaving the company." As much thinking and rehearsing as Patrick had done for this moment, it sure came out easy and simple. Four words.

"What? Leaving? Nonsense," Linda said.

"It's true," Patrick said, answering his mother, but unable to tear his eyes away from his father. "I'm resigning my position, effective immediately."

She pulled her spine up straight. "It's really very selfish of you, Patrick, to choose tonight of all nights to spring this nonsense on us."

"It's not nonsense. It's long overdue. And it's happening."

His father's eyebrows were knit very close together. But it wasn't an angry scowl. More like a scowl of concentration, as if he was studying a specimen under a microscope, trying to understand it. Oddly, Patrick felt…seen.

"Is this about a woman?" Linda asked. "That woman you were cavorting around with up in the mountains?"

Patrick sighed. "We weren't cavorting, Mother. We were saving a girl's life. It was very harrowing. And, no, this isn't completely about her. But it is partially about her."

She rolled her eyes. "That doesn't make any sense."

"I know," he said. "I don't have passion for real estate. You both know this. You've always known it." His father nodded slowly. "I took the job because I felt so guilty about Hannah. But it's never been what I want in my life. Hannah's gone, but I'm still here."

"And what will you do? Climb mountains for a living?" his mother asked.

"There are worse things. I have money. I could open a ski school."

To this, his mother balked out loud.

"You know I could," Patrick insisted. "I'm a good skier."

"Tell that to your dead sister," Linda said bitterly.

"That's enough, Linda." Pat Rogers had finally spoken, but his eyes still had never left his son. "What happened to Hannah was an accident. And it was as much her fault as Patrick's."

"How could you…?"

"It doesn't make us love her any less," Pat said, finally directing his attention to her. "But you've spent every day since then holding a grudge against your son and making him feel like you love him less."

"That's ridiculous. I don't love you less, Patrick," she said. "You know that."

"I do know that," Patrick said. "And I think that's why I took the job in the first place. I was trying to make you happy with me. But now I have to worry about what makes me happy. Real estate doesn't make me happy."

"Believe it or not, I've been waiting for this for some time," Pat said. "Pretty much since you took the job. I'm glad you're finally leaving the company. You're great at what you do, and we will miss your work. But real estate is not who you are. I'm glad to see you come to that realization and do something about it, son. Your mother and I are here to support you in whatever way you need."

"Thanks, Dad," Patrick said, awash with relief, as if the greatest weight had been lifted from him.

And when his mother stood and gave him a stiff hug, he took it for what it was—the first hug he'd received from her since before he and Hannah went up on that mountain. In many ways, he would cherish that hug. It meant progress. Once upon a time, he would have thought that nothing he could say would change anything between them. But he'd laid it all out there, and sometimes that was exactly what it took to get the necessary results.

They went back to the party, each going their separate ways. As promised, Patrick chatted with Ellie, and he made the effort to say hello to his grandparents. But with those tasks, and the most important task, complete, he really didn't see any reason to stay. He stopped at Hannah's photo again, gave her a quick nod and said, "I did it. I got my life back. I know you'd want that."

And he was certain that was true—she would have wanted that for him. Hannah was a generous and kind person.

But he also knew quitting Rogers Real Estate wouldn't have been all she wanted for him. He knew he still had work to do.

He left the party quietly and made the long walk back to his car. He had to get back to Gorham.

He had to get to Erin.

Chapter Twenty-Four

In Erin's world, reporters hanging around meant something tragic had happened. The sight of a news van made her tense. On the day they'd rescued Kerrington, she'd expected news coverage to be waiting at the base of the mountain. But she was nowhere near prepared for the deluge of reporters who'd scurried about for a solid week after the rescue, calling them heroes, asking questions, snapping photos.

Kerrington's kidnapping, and her triumphant return, was a national story.

It was nice being a hero, but it also felt weird. It made her think of all the times they failed to get someone down safely. It wasn't often, but when it happened, it was seared into Erin's memory for all time.

She and Patrick hadn't spoken since that day. Rebbie told her that he'd gone home to New Castle and was taking a break from climbing. Erin couldn't blame him, although she missed him. And while she'd prepared for an onslaught of curious hikers to get themselves stranded trying to find the cabin where

Kerrington had been held, it never happened. She supposed those were the type of thrill seekers who would wait until summer's warmth.

The weather stayed nasty for two solid weeks. Other than when she'd gotten the flu during her junior year of college, it was the longest Erin went without climbing. Her arms and legs had healed from the bumps and bruises, and were restless for use. She felt incomplete.

Finally, there was a break in the weather. The sun came out and the temperatures rose just slightly. The Realtor arrived, right on time, and Erin let her inside.

"It's a beautiful one out there," she chirped, hauling her giant purse to the kitchen table. "A bit cold, but what can you expect around here in the winter? I consider it a selling point." She winked. "Cold weather, no mosquitos. You ready to sign some paperwork and get this ball rolling?"

"It's good to see the sun," Erin said half-heartedly. She was not at all excited to sign paperwork. She didn't want to get anything rolling. The clouds may have broken outside, but in her heart, it was still gray and gloomy.

"I hear you're a real hometown hero," the Realtor said as she pulled off her gloves, one finger at a time.

"I don't know about that," Erin said. "I was just doing my job."

"That's not what I read. I read that you overcame all sorts of obstacles up there."

"There were a few," Erin agreed. If only she knew what obstacles Erin had really overcome. And what new obstacles stood in her way because of it.

"I saw a picture of the man you were up there with. That's what I call a mountain view." She had begun pulling file folders out of her bag and laying them on the table.

Erin chuckled. "He was amazing. I couldn't have done it without him."

"Sounds like you guys had a real rapport. A good thing for that girl." She held out a pen for Erin to take.

"Yeah," Erin said slowly, too busy recalling the tender moments with Patrick inside the chapel that night to take the pen. "We had a rapport. We got each other."

"Aw-w-w," the Realtor said, placing her hand over her heart. "That kind of connection is so wonderful, isn't it?"

Erin smiled. "Yes, it is."

"And rare." She shook the pen a little. "You ready to get started?"

Ten minutes later, it was done. Over. Time to move forward and move on. Fresh start and all that.

The weather was beautiful. Erin's mind was finally clear, and she longed to sink her spikes into the mountain. She grabbed her gear and drove to PARR.

Rebbie was sitting at the desk when Erin came inside.

"Hey," Erin said, pulling off her stocking cap and gloves. She reached for the coffeepot. "Why are you here today? Is there a rescue?"

Rebbie nodded, not looking up from whatever she was working on.

"Where?"

"Right here," Rebbie said.

Erin craned to look out the window. "Right where? What does that mean, 'right here'?"

Rebbie put down her pencil and took off her glasses, letting them drop to the end of their lanyard. "Right here in this office," she said. "You're the rescue."

Erin smiled, thinking this was surely a joke. "Me? How so?"

"You think I can't tell, but I've known you a long time, Erin Hadaway. You are in love, and you're trying not to be."

"Oh, come on now," Erin said, but she ducked away so Rebbie couldn't see her face, which felt flushed.

Rebbie stood. "'Oh, come on now' is my line." She came around her desk and gently held Erin's arms so she was forced to look directly at Rebbie. "What is so wrong with being in love?"

"Nothing is wrong with it," Erin said. "But you've had me in love with every available man since you started working here."

"I have not," Rebbie said. "Yes, I've wanted to get you interested in love. I've wanted you to meet the man of your dreams. It's just that now I think you actually have."

"If you'll recall, you thought he was the man of my dreams before I even met him. You'd only known him a few minutes yourself."

"And that was all I needed to know. And I was right."

Erin gently pulled out of Rebbie's grasp and took a sip of her coffee to hide the goofy smirk she couldn't seem to keep at bay.

"What more could you want from a man?" Rebbie

asked. "He's good-looking and charming and sweet and an actual hero. You two are perfect for each other."

"I know," Erin said.

Rebbie did a double take. "Excuse me, did you just say—"

Erin nodded. "I know. But we've already decided we're not going to go there."

"Why on earth not?"

Erin could have explained about the house and the Realtor and Patrick's development project and his insistence on staying in Gorham. She could have talked all day about the unfairness of her finally finding someone who literally understood exactly everything she'd felt about losing Jason and not being able to be with him. She could have told her about the respect they'd each gained for the other on that mountain, and her desperation as she dug through the snow, begging God to not let her lose him.

But really, she just wanted to climb.

"Rebbie, you're the sweetest friend, do you know that?" She kissed her friend on the cheek, then went to the little closet and pulled down a snowsuit. She'd left her old one up on the mountain and had never gone back to retrieve it. She was pretty sure she could climb right to it, if she wanted to get it back. But she wasn't sure she was ready to make that climb yet.

Hills first, then mountains.

"Don't try to change the subject," Rebbie countered.

"I am changing the subject, though." Erin climbed into her suit and grabbed a backpack. She pawed through to make sure it had everything she needed, then shrugged into it. "I love you for looking out for me. But trust me, I've got this."

She patted Rebbie twice on the shoulder, grabbed her truck keys and headed out.

When she got to her truck, she paused and looked over the beautiful, dangerous range.

It was time to say goodbye.

Chapter Twenty-Five

Rebbie was just getting ready to close up the PARR office when Patrick arrived. She took one look at him, squealed and launched into a hug.

"I thought you were never coming back!" she said into his shoulder.

He patted her back and laughed. "You can't get rid of me that easily."

She pulled away. "Are you good? Like, *good* good?"

He flexed a muscle. "Good-good as new-new."

"That whole thing was crazy. You probably won't believe me when I tell you it's never happened before."

"I would find it much harder to believe if you told me it happened every weekend," he said. "I might have to hit the gym a little more often if that's the case. That was exhausting."

"I'm sure it was. All I know is you two are the recipients of a lot of prayer. A lot of *answered* prayer."

"And we appreciate it. Speaking of us two...where is the other one?"

"Erin? Oh." Rebbie gestured toward the mountain.

His eyebrows shot up. He didn't know why this surprised him; he supposed he just thought it would be a while longer before she'd be ready to go up again. "By herself?"

"Yeah. Against her own new rule, I might add. I will say she was a little off today. Not in a bad way. She seemed to be in a good mood. I just had a sense there was something going on with her."

"Did she take the traverse?"

Rebbie shrugged. "I can look on the GPS if you'd like."

He winced. "Would you mind?"

"Not at all." Rebbie went back to her desk and shook her mouse to wake her computer monitor. She studied it for a minute. "Looks like she's headed toward... Tuckerman's? That's weird. She never goes up there. Usually avoids it like the plague. See, I told you she was off."

"Tuckerman Ravine?"

She nodded. "It's sort of a haunted place for her. For all of us."

"She told me all about it."

This time it was Rebbie's turn to look surprised. "She talked about Jason? She never talks about him. Always avoids the subject. Just like she avoids the ravine."

"We had lots of time to share," he said. "We have... things in common." He could feel Rebbie take this in, deciding whether or not to pry.

"Can I ask you a question?" Rebbie tilted her head to one side.

"Sure."

"Are you in love with her?"

Patrick paused. Not exactly the type of prying he was expecting.

"We hardly know each other."

"I didn't ask if you knew her favorite pasta and the name of her third-grade teacher. I asked if you're in love with her."

It wasn't that he didn't know the answer. It was that this would be the first time he would admit it out loud in no uncertain terms. It was going to make it truer. It would be harder to shield himself from pain once he said it.

But the pain of not saying it would be far worse.

"Desperately."

Rebbie gave a triumphant little jump and fist pump. "I knew it! I knew! And I'm telling you, I think she's in love with you, too. The two of you are made for each— What are you doing?"

Patrick had moved to the closet and was looking for a snowsuit that might fit him. He found one—navy blue—and climbed inside it.

"I'm going up to Tuckerman Ravine."

"You can't do that by yourself. The new rule."

"Obviously, she's okay with breaking a rule or two."

"You're still in training." But Rebbie's grin, which she held behind tented fingers, took the seriousness out of her admonishment. It was a grin that said, "Who am I to stand in the way of true love?"

He zipped up and pulled a gaiter over his head, then

reached for one of the spare backpacks in the back of the closet. "Training or not, I love Erin, and I have to tell her before it's too late."

Chapter Twenty-Six

Erin sat on a boulder overlooking the ravine. There was something about the stretch of untouched snow that made her want to run down it, be the first person to plant footprints there, like the first person to walk on the moon.

She was mesmerized by the snow arch, the sun bouncing off it and making it glisten and shimmer like jewels. She could understand what would drive a tourist up here to see it. How magical it would feel to be inside that arch.

This was the first time she'd been at Tucks since Jason died. She hadn't spent a ton of time there before his death. It was dangerous, and when things went wrong, they often did so tragically. She was compelled to go up because she needed to say goodbye. But now, once she was up here, the words didn't want to come. She only wanted to stare and think about friendship and drink in the beauty.

At least Jason had died somewhere beautiful. At least his last sights on this earth were of God's glory.

The thought didn't make her feel a lot better, but maybe a little.

She heard a crunch of snow behind her and whipped around. Part of her remained haunted by the man she'd left at the bottom of the cliff over on the Madison and the body of his son, who she'd left partially buried under the snow by the cabin. The sheriff had brought in another rescue group to help them recover those bodies, so she knew they were no longer here. But that didn't make her any less jumpy.

The figure she saw crunching up the snowy ravine was no bad guy. It was Patrick, wearing another of Jason's snowsuits and taking each step very, very cautiously. She stood and shaded her eyes while she watched him approach. The sight of him made her happy and warm.

When he got close enough, she called out. "What are you doing here?"

"Hyperventilating, mostly," he panted. "I think adrenaline kept me from realizing how exhausting this was the last time we were up here."

Erin giggled. "You get used to it." She waited for him to close the gap, then made room for him on the rock.

He stayed standing, though, taking in a long view of the ravine. "So this is it, huh?"

She pointed at the snow arch. "Over there."

"I thought it collapsed."

"They rebuild. This one's much smaller. Would have been much easier to dig out of."

Finally, Patrick sat, his shoulder brushing up against hers. Erin thought that maybe the next time she saw or talked to Patrick, it would be awkward. Taken out of their dire situation, they might find that their first impressions about each other were actually right. They might discover they didn't have anything in common, after all. They might not feel the pull of attraction.

But she did feel it. And she knew that not only did they have something in common, but what did bind them was also the deepest parts of themselves. And it wasn't awkward. It was almost as if they were picking up on a conversation that had merely been interrupted for a few minutes. Patrick was exciting and comfortable, all at the same time.

"You never answered my question," she said. "What are you doing up here?"

"What are you doing up here?" he countered.

She glanced at the arch again. "Saying goodbye."

"Ah." He nodded, looking at his boots, and if Erin didn't know better, she would have said it was a resigned nod. "Then it really doesn't matter what I'm doing up here, because I'm doing it too late. I was trying to avoid that."

"Avoid me saying goodbye?"

"It's something I never want to hear from you."

"But I'm not saying goodbye to you."

"Not yet." He paused, never taking his eyes off the arch. "I said goodbye myself last week. Something I never thought I'd do."

Erin shook her head. "I don't understand. Who did you say goodbye to?"

"Rogers Real Estate Development, LLC." He finally met her eyes. "I quit."

"You quit? Why?"

He sighed. "Well, because a wise woman I know once told me that what happened with my sister wasn't my fault and that I should follow my dreams, not what's expected of me. She was right."

Erin smiled. "She sounds very wise."

"The wisest."

It felt as if the air was packed full of unsaid words. Just feelings on top of feelings on top of feelings, everything getting jammed up into a big, impenetrable cloud. She could hear Rebbie in her head, screaming at her to just say things already. Make it happen. Stop being so cautious all the time. But every second that ticked by without her opening her mouth felt like a lost opportunity.

"So you're saying goodbye," Patrick said.

"It's long overdue. I figured the longer I held on to—"

"I also quit because I love you."

He said it so matter-of-factly, Erin wasn't quite sure she'd heard it correctly. She blinked, afraid he'd said something else and she'd only heard "I love you" because it was what she wanted to hear.

"You…what?"

"I quit because I love you and I want to be with you. And I know you want to leave this mountain, and I want to stay. But I don't want to stay if you're not here. I want to be able to go wherever you go. If… you want me to, of course."

She realized she was holding her breath and then let it out slowly. "I don't," she whispered, and then kicked herself for saying the exact wrong thing.

His face clouded over. "You…don't. Okay. Well, that changes things."

She shook her head. "No, what I mean is… I don't want you to follow me anywhere because I'm not going anywhere."

"You said you're up here to say goodbye."

"I'm saying goodbye to Jason and this accident and my guilt. I needed to put it all to rest. This ravine and that arch and the people who died here. I needed to let myself accept that his death was an accident and I had no idea it would happen, or I would have done anything I could to prevent it. But even if I had come up here with him, I have no doubt I would have been inside that arch with him. He still would have died, and I would have, too."

"So you're not leaving?"

She shook her head. "I couldn't. Not if it meant leaving you. I told the Realtor this morning that I didn't want to sell. Refused to sign the paperwork. I love you, Patrick. You are my home."

His smile sent chills through Erin. He reached over and cupped the back of her neck with his hand. "Say it again."

"I love you, Patrick Rogers," she said. "And I'm staying here to be with you."

"I love you, Erin Hadaway. And I couldn't be happier."

In the midst of all that snow and ice and cold, cold wind, they melted into a kiss.

Chapter Twenty-Seven

"That was terrifying," Rebbie said as she settled onto a little wooden pew. Her purple sequined snow boots perfectly matched the flowers on her dress. "I truly thought I was going to fall out of that thing."

"You're being dramatic," Tommy said, dropping down next to her, a guilty half smile in place. "A few little jokes and you're all drama."

"You don't joke while flying a helicopter, Tommy. You give your passengers heart palpitations with your little jokes. I still haven't decided if I'm willing to ride with you back down."

"It's either that or you live here now," he said. "Because I don't see you getting a whole lot of climbing done in that dress and those boots."

"I had to wear a dress. It's a wedding."

"It's a wedding that *you* orchestrated," Erin said, cutting in. "So you shouldn't bicker while you're here."

"Oh, you know it's all good fun," Tommy said, wrapping his arm around Rebbie and pulling her in for a friendly hug. "She loved every minute of my taxi service."

"One of these days, I'm going to fire you," Rebbie said, but she was all smiles as she leaned into his shoulder. "Now, stop, you're going to flatten my hair. I can hardly believe it didn't all fall out from fear."

"Where are the other passengers?" Erin asked.

"They were doing some looking around before the ceremony starts," Tommy said.

"I think they were trying to see the cabin from here," Rebbie said. "They saw it from the sky."

"I'm sure that wasn't easy," Patrick said, adjusting his cuffs.

"Sure ended Mr. Jokester's little anecdotes right away," Rebbie said, casting another playful glare at Tommy, who stared at his shoes, remorseful.

"I wasn't even thinking about that," he said.

Patrick reached out and patted his shoulder. "Aw, it's all right, Tommy. No harm done in trying to have a little fun. If it makes you feel any better, my ride up here was smooth sailing."

"Thanks," Tommy said.

Rebbie gave Tommy a light sock in the shoulder. "You didn't tease Patrick, but you teased me?"

Tommy shrugged. "You're more fun to tease."

Patrick looked absolutely adorable in his tux, Erin thought. Crisp and clean-shaven, his bow tie perfectly straight and his shoes perfectly shined. He'd ditched the climbing clothes, and the climb, for this. And here she was in a big orange snowsuit.

Little did he know, the suit was covering up a white lace gown, simple enough to hide inside a snowsuit,

elegant enough to take his breath away when she un-
veiled it. Rebbie had thought of everything. She and
Erin had spent half an hour that morning artfully rolling up the gown so it wouldn't wrinkle and so it would
fall just-so when the suit was unzipped.

"It'll be like a Cinderella situation," Rebbie had
said. "All you need is some talking mice. You should
twirl while it's happening."

Erin had laughed. "I'd prefer no mice at my wedding, thank you. And I'm not much of a twirler."

But Rebbie was right—the gown was perfect for
twirling. Erin had secretly twirled in front of her
bedroom mirror several times. She loved the way it
swished heavily against her ankles when she stopped.

"Besides," she'd added, "there's no room for twirling in that chapel, anyway."

Of course, they were going to marry in the tiny
chapel hidden in the notch. They'd visited it so many
times since Kerrington's rescue, they'd begun to think
of it as their spot. Although, secretly, Erin had thought
of it as their spot since that cold, frightening night
when they'd leaned on each other and on their faith
to get them through.

The last few times they'd come up, they'd tucked
cleaning supplies and ribbon into Erin's backpack
and, bit by bit, cleaned it top to bottom. Once all the
cobwebs had been knocked down and the pews all
dusted, they'd hung simple white bows on the backs
of the pews and set some white taper candles on the
altar. Falling in love was almost never easy, and their
journey to each other had been anything but. They'd
agreed that the wedding should be simple. Just a few

decorations and a few guests. Their love would be their decor.

Tommy's first trip had brought the bride and groom, plus Pastor Elmer, Roberta and Patrick's parents. Erin's parents couldn't make the trip, so after the ceremony, they were going to load up and travel down to Kentucky, where Patrick would meet the Hadaway clan for the first time.

While they finished sprucing up, Tommy had gone back down to pick up the second load of passengers— Rebbie, Kerrington Hadley and her parents. They were the guests of honor.

Kerrington's parents had been hesitant to accept the invitation, which Patrick and Erin formally extended in person while drinking tea and eating shortbread cookies at their gleaming dining room table in their sprawling mansion in New Castle. They knew Patrick and Erin and were incredibly grateful to them for what they'd done. They'd invited them to celebrate Kerrington's birthday, and even invited them to stop by for a visit at Christmas. But going up into the mountain where their daughter had been held captive was pushing the limits of what they could bear.

Kerrington, however, had jumped right on the opportunity, begging them to please let her go. So they'd agreed to come, too.

The chapel door opened, and the little family shuffled inside. Erin was pretty sure Kerrington's mother had been crying, but Kerrington looked exhilarated and pink and excited. Erin knew it had taken Kerrington a lot of time and patience to get to the place where she was, and she hadn't just achieved healing, but a zest for life that Erin sometimes envied. Kerrington bounded to the front of the chapel and nearly bowled over Erin with a hug.

"Congratulations, Mrs. Rogers!"

Erin laughed and squeezed Kerrington tight. "Not yet! But thank you."

Mrs. Hadley stood by with tears in her eyes, and Mr. Hadley shook Patrick's hand. Kerrington stepped back and gave Erin a once-over.

"You're wearing that?" she asked.

"I was just thinking the same thing," Roberta said. "Not that you don't look lovely, dear."

"Not exactly," Erin said. She gave Rebbie a little wink and nod, and Rebbie jumped up and scuffled over to help Erin unzip. The dress unfurled just as they planned, making everyone in the chapel gasp. If Erin was being honest, it did feel a little like a Cinderella moment, and Rebbie was her fairy godmother. What an excellent fairy godmother she would make.

Rebbie spent a minute fluffing Erin's hair and whispered, "Gorgeous," then kissed her on the cheek and sat back down.

Erin found herself face-to-face with Patrick, who looked as if he'd just stumbled upon a cache of rare gems.

"You look stunning," he whispered. "What did I do to deserve this? I have the most beautiful wife in the world."

"Not yet, you don't," Pastor Elmer whispered, and everyone laughed. "Should we get started?"

Patrick held out his hand, and Erin took it. Together, they took the few short steps to the front of the chapel, while the Hadleys slid into seats. The stained-glass windows threw prisms over the cross above Pastor Elmer. He opened his Bible and started reading.

The ceremony was lovely—the pastor's words perfect—and while they all sang "Bind Us Together," Erin couldn't help thinking about what did bind the two of them. At first, it had seemed like grief and guilt. But over time, she realized they'd been bound together by something much deeper. Acceptance. Faith. Resilience. Trust. It was almost as if they'd been bound long before they even knew each other.

Erin held Patrick's hands and looked deep into his eyes as he recited his vows to her. She never wanted to forget this moment and was sure she'd never be able to, even if she tried.

He shifted from foot to foot nervously. It was adorable. "Erin, when we came up this mountain, we both had bigger mountains to get over. Mountains we thought we'd never see the bottom of again. And, I'll admit, I was a little scared of you." He paused while everyone chuckled. "But it didn't take long. I knew the minute we stood on Tuna Tears Rock—" Rebbie let out a snort, sending the whole group into chuckles again. "I knew long before we got to this chapel that you were the reason I was here. Not just here on this mountain, but here on this earth. You are so brave, and so loyal, and I definitely never want to get into an arm-wrestling competition with you." More chuckles, and then he got serious, emotional. "And you rescued me, Erin. I knew you had rescued me when my greatest fear stopped being about facing the past and turned into facing a possible future without you. I promise to climb all of life's mountains with you, wherever and whatever that means."

When it was Erin's turn, she was so overcome with emotion, she could barely speak. Everything they'd been through together coursed through his hands into hers, history and future all rolled into one, making her feel hopeful and excited and deeply, deeply loved.

"When Rebbie told me I was about to meet the man of my dreams, she had no idea how right she was."

"Yes, I did," Rebbie said, and again there was laughter.

"Okay, she probably did. But I didn't. Patrick, I was asleep before I met you. I was sleeping and refusing to wake up because I was afraid of pain. But you showed me how to wake up, and *why* to wake up. And there you were. A dream, come to life. And you did this, thinking we would never be together. You loved me enough to let me go, and that's something I will never forget. The thing is, once I woke up, I couldn't go. There was no way. Going would mean leaving behind the best thing that's ever happened to me. You say I rescued you, but you rescued me. We rescued each other. And I want to keep doing that for the rest of our lives. I made a promise to you that we would come down this mountain together. I still make that promise. This mountain, and every other mountain we might face."

When the ceremony was over, Rebbie rushed to the helicopter and came back with a cake. They moved the pews so everyone was in a big circle, and they ate cake and laughed and told stories and laughed some more. Erin found herself staring at the cross above the altar—the one she and Patrick both leaned on during their long night of waiting and wondering and doubting and sharing and falling. Everything good that had come to her had come from faith. It was no coincidence she'd found this little chapel tucked away in a notch in the midst of this enormous mountain range.

This chapel was much more than a pit stop, shelter from the cold and wind.

This chapel was home.

This mountain was home.

And she was never going to leave it.

Epilogue

It had been a while since Erin had trained anyone. That had long since been taken over by others. Rich had trained Tiffany, who in turn trained Joseph, who trained Riley, who trained both Dennis and Tara. On and on, a PARR chain. Rescuers drifted in and out like the tide, and Erin found herself letting go a little bit, finishing her coffee and the morning news if someone else was available to take the call.

Patrick became one of PARR's best and most dedicated rescuers, next to Erin. But once the resort took off, his duties there had pulled him away from rescuing, and Erin couldn't possibly ask him to forgo his dream in order to help out a rescue group that didn't really need it, anyway.

Also, he was a true ripper on the slopes. He hadn't been exaggerating about that. He could go down with the same adeptness that she could go up. And he was an astonishingly good instructor. Safety was his number-one goal.

Often, Erin worked the desk while he taught. She met people from all over the world, including plenty of true crime fans who wanted to see the mountain where the famous Kerrington Hadley had been kept by kidnappers. Erin was puzzled by their morbid curiosity, but she didn't fight it. In fact, there were so many rescues on the infamous cliff, she'd installed permanent anchors to make it easier on them.

PARR training had a heavy focus on the area surrounding the cabin.

So, of course, that was where she started her training today.

"Okay, we're going to go up this cliff," she said, stepping into her harness and checking her trainee's to make sure everything was secure. He had a long way to go before he would be fully trained and ready to join PARR, but he had to start somewhere. "I'm going up first. If you run into any trouble, just yell, or tug the rope, or both. Watch where I put my hands and feet and follow." She adjusted her helmet. "I've been up this cliff more times than I can count, and I can assure you the way I'm going up is the best and easiest way. Whatever you do, don't get fancy. Remember, we're here for rescue purposes, not for showing off."

With that, she set upon the cliff.

It never failed. As soon as she slipped her fingers into the first crack, she would be blasted back in time. Her heartbeat would speed up, and her breath would come more quickly. She'd have a sense of someone behind her, and she would feel a need to get up this cliff as fast as humanly possible.

Then she would remember Patrick. How he'd been behind her, fearlessly climbing, trusting her, trusting himself. Still to this day, she would never know how an inexperienced climber had ascended that cliff face so perfectly, and in record time.

Sometimes, God was just on your side.

She had to go much slower this time. Not everyone was Patrick. Of course, not everyone was being chased, either.

When she got to the top of the cliff, she turned and helped pull up her trainee, just as she'd done with Patrick that day. It was an eerie sense of déjà vu that delighted her.

"So where is it?" the trainee asked.

"Be patient, catch your breath. It's just over there." She pointed to the ledge where she and Patrick had watched over the cabin. The ledge where she'd taunted the kidnapper to come get her.

Now there was a railing there. She'd installed it herself after one too many curiosity-seekers had fallen and been severely injured. The railing was covered with notes written directly onto the wood. Not an aesthetic she really loved, but the messages were for Kerrington, and all were lovely. She could hardly argue with that.

"Whoa, you and Dad sat on this ledge with no railing?"

She smiled. "We did. And he was so brave, he actually went off that way to get back down to the cabin, and I went the other way and continued going up."

Her ten-year-old son's eyes were saucers as he

gazed around him, the story he had heard since he was a toddler finally coming to life for him.

"It's weird to see the resort from up here," he said. "Especially to think the cabin was all that was there when you guys did this."

"Very weird," she said. The cabin was now just a small part of the lobby of KH Cabin Ski Resort. They'd spent a lifetime building around it, creating a luxury lodge with a dozen rooms and a renowned ski school. "But not as weird as standing up here next to my baby looking down at it." She gave him a quick side-hug.

She was so proud of her son. Patrick Harold Rogers IV—Patty, as they called him—was the best of both of them. He was funny and kind like his father, and fearless and driven like his mother. It seemed like the minute he took his first step, Erin was constantly pulling him off of and out of precarious places. He loved the mountain. Like he was born for it. He had been asking to join PARR for years. By the time he was of age, he would likely be better at climbing than both of them combined.

"You must have been really scared," Patty said.

"We were," Erin admitted. "But we had faith and we had each other. We were blessed that it all worked out."

"So was Auntie Kerrington."

"Auntie Kerrington is amazing because she can see what happened to her as a blessing. Many people wouldn't have."

"Do you think you and Dad would have fallen in

love if it weren't for that kidnapping?" He rubbed his thumb over the words *We Love You*.

Erin thought about it. What a life she and Patrick had lived. It was everything both of them had dreamed it would be. Something so perfect, it shouldn't be real. They were soul mates in every possible way.

"I do," she said. "I don't know where or when or how, because our lives were so different. But I do believe we still would have found each other."

"Me, too," he said.

Erin pulled out her water bottle and Patty did the same. They drank and silently watched skiers go up the ridge and down again.

"Are you ready?" she asked. "I have someplace else I want to show you."

He finished his water and tucked the empty bottle back into his pack. "Where?"

"It's a tiny chapel hidden in the notch," she said. "It's where Dad and I got married. It's a very important place to us."

"Sure," he said. "But I want to take lead this time."

Erin paused, sizing him up. He was a young man now, the spitting image of his father. He saw the world through the lens of adventure. It made him a little difficult to keep up with at times, and he'd given Erin more worries than she could count. But it was that same optimism, that same eagerness to enjoy God's creations, that drew people to him. Erin would admit to getting caught up in it herself.

"Okay," she said. "Just watch your footing and be careful. Take it slow!" But he was already scrambling up the cliff face before she could finish her warning. She gave the rope some slack and shook her head, chuckling. She tipped up her face to watch him go. He made it look so effortless. "I swear you have hooves, son! Hooves!"

* * * * *

LOVE INSPIRED

Stories to uplift and inspire

Fall in love with Love Inspired—
inspirational and uplifting stories of faith
and hope. Find strength and comfort in
the bonds of friendship and community.
Revel in the warmth of possibility and the
promise of new beginnings.

Sign up for the Love Inspired newsletter
at **LoveInspired.com** to be the first
to find out about upcoming titles,
special promotions and exclusive content.

CONNECT WITH US AT:

Facebook.com/LoveInspiredBooks

Twitter.com/LoveInspiredBks

Get 4 FREE REWARDS!

We'll send you 2 FREE Books plus 2 FREE Mystery Gifts.

FREE Value Over **$20**

Both the **Love Inspired**® and **Love Inspired**® Suspense series feature compelling novels filled with inspirational romance, faith, forgiveness, and hope.

YES! Please send me 2 FREE novels from the Love Inspired or Love Inspired Suspense series and my 2 FREE gifts (gifts are worth about $10 retail). After receiving them, if I don't wish to receive any more books, I can return the shipping statement marked "cancel." If I don't cancel, I will receive 6 brand-new Love Inspired Larger-Print books or Love Inspired Suspense Larger-Print books every month and be billed just $6.24 each in the U.S. or $6.49 each in Canada. That is a savings of at least 17% off the cover price. It's quite a bargain! Shipping and handling is just 50¢ per book in the U.S. and $1.25 per book in Canada.* I understand that accepting the 2 free books and gifts places me under no obligation to buy anything. I can always return a shipment and cancel at any time by calling the number below. The free books and gifts are mine to keep no matter what I decide.

Choose one: ☐ **Love Inspired**
Larger-Print
(122/322 IDN GRDF)

☐ **Love Inspired Suspense**
Larger-Print
(107/307 IDN GRDF)

Name (please print)

Address   Apt. #

City   State/Province   Zip/Postal Code

Email: Please check this box ☐ if you would like to receive newsletters and promotional emails from Harlequin Enterprises ULC and its affiliates. You can unsubscribe anytime.

Mail to the **Harlequin Reader Service:**
IN U.S.A.: P.O. Box 1341, Buffalo, NY 14240-8531
IN CANADA: P.O. Box 603, Fort Erie, Ontario L2A 5X3

Want to try 2 free books from another series? Call 1-800-873-8635 or visit www.ReaderService.com.

*Terms and prices subject to change without notice. Prices do not include sales taxes, which will be charged (if applicable) based on your state or country of residence. Canadian residents will be charged applicable taxes. Offer not valid in Quebec. This offer is limited to one order per household. Books received may not be as shown. Not valid for current subscribers to the Love Inspired or Love Inspired Suspense series. All orders subject to approval. Credit or debit balances in a customer's account(s) may be offset by any other outstanding balance owed by or to the customer. Please allow 4 to 6 weeks for delivery. Offer available while quantities last.

Your Privacy—Your information is being collected by Harlequin Enterprises ULC, operating as Harlequin Reader Service. For a complete summary of the information we collect, how we use this information and to whom it is disclosed, please visit our privacy notice located at corporate.harlequin.com/privacy-notice. From time to time we may also exchange your personal information with reputable third parties. If you wish to opt out of this sharing of your personal information, please visit readerservice.com/consumerschoice or call 1-800-873-8635. **Notice to California Residents**—Under California law, you have specific rights to control and access your data. For more information on these rights and how to exercise them, visit corporate.harlequin.com/california-privacy.

LIRLIS22R2

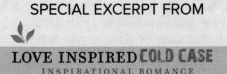
Detective Snyder strode into the coffee shop. His broad
shoulders anchored a fit man with dark hair and dark eyes.
Looking to be just over six feet tall, he filled the doorway.
His sunglasses hid whatever he was thinking, which Kate
was pretty sure began and ended with the words *annoying
woman*.

He slid onto one of the bar stools and set a folder beside
him. He had a nice profile, she realized, with sharp features
dominated by his chocolate-brown eyes. In another life, he
might be the kind of guy she'd date, but in this life, she was
too consumed with righting the wrongs of her small town to
even consider dating someone.

"Is that my folder?" she asked.

"You get right down to business, I see." A smile flickered
on his face. "That's one thing we have in common."

"When a missing girl needs to be found, whether someone
took her or...worse, I don't want to waste a second."

His smile evaporated. Clearly, he didn't like her questioning
the police department's conclusions about what had happened

to Lily Ridge. Maybe it was because his father had been the one to do the initial investigation.

"I don't think you're going to find any surprises in there," he said. "The case is open-and-shut."

She took the folder from him and began flipping through the file. Several lines were blacked out. Frustration welled in her chest. "If Lily's case is so open-and-shut, why isn't everything here?"

"Because we're protecting the privacy of citizens."

"Oh come on, Detective. Why are you protecting anyone's identity if they would corroborate your version of the story?"

He bristled. "There are no versions, Ms. McAllister. There is only the truth, and the truth is that Lily Ridge left home on purpose."

Kate couldn't believe that the girl had just run off without a word to her parents for three years. Everyone she'd talked to had said Lily wasn't the kind of girl to do that.

He continued: "The case is three years old and has already been closed. There is no need to go chasing rabbits down trails that lead nowhere." He got to his feet. "Thank you for the coffee, ma'am."

The detective dropped a few dollars on the counter, then left the shop. Kate clutched the folder to her chest and vowed that Detective Snyder was not going to have the last word on Lily Ridge. The girl was out there somewhere, and it was up to Kate to bring her home. No matter how much effort that took or where the trail led her...

Don't miss After She Vanished *by Shirley Jump, available wherever Love Inspired books and ebooks are sold August 23, 2022.*

LoveInspired.com

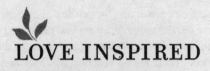